The Adventures of Jake & Archie

Table of Contents

Written By
J.R. Wilson

The Adventures of
Jake & Archie

Written By
J.R. Wilson

The Adventures of
Jake & Archie

Acknowledgement

I would like to thank the following folks for helping get this book off the ground. You're invaluable. I can't Thank you enough!

My wife Pamela, James Wilson Jr, Gilbert Wilson, April Erickson, Christine Wilson, Natalie Wilson, and of course Aubrey Joy Wilson.

Written By
J.R. Wilson

The Adventures of
Jake & Archie

Written By
J.R. Wilson

The Adventures of
Jake & Archie

Introduction

This is a story told by a small-town country boy. It is about a retired Navy Seal who ran Black Ops for twenty-five years. His wife June and some of his buddies from the service, who live on his ranch he inherited in Colorado. The adventures start there when two aliens decide to fight and crash over their ranch. Life is never going to be the same. Jake and his boys and sometimes his wife have adventures in space and make alliances with some aliens and battle others. The action pauses but never really stops. I hope you enjoy reading. You will enjoy Archie, I won't spoil the story. Thanks for reading my book.

Written By
J.R. Wilson

The Adventures of
Jake & Archie

Written By
J.R. Wilson

The Adventures of
Jake & Archie

Chapter 1
Unwanted Visitor

This is a most unusual story; it's not a love story and it's not a who done it. It's about a six-foot two retired navy seal, and a few of his squad who retired with him. He ran a squad of black ops and after twenty-five years, his wife, who has been with him since high school and Jake decided it was time. So they all live on a ranch in Colorado that he inherited. June and Jake were high school sweethearts. June is about five foot seven and very pretty she is pushing fifty but looks like she's in her late 30's, light brown hair. June is a pistol she's tuff but loving. Jake is fifty-two, well-built and fit a former seal commander, so you know he's in shape he let his hair grow out some, no more, high and tight. Their two sons are in the military. Tony was a six foot three a Navy Seal. Jamie is a six-foot four marine. Both have brown hair and a lot like their dad.

We open with two space fighters going head-to-head and slipping from one galaxy to another. When they slipped through the last one and ended up just above earth they fired and hit each

Written By
J.R. Wilson

other, The Gruller ship was headed towards earth the pilot and navigator beamed out and ended up on Jake and Junes ranch. The Amorlite ship was falling apart, and the Navigator was hurt so they also beamed out to the surface.

Jake and June are sitting on their front porch, it's a nice evening, very warm for Colorado. June suggested," How about a hot rum toddy old man."

"Old! I'm not old I'm just coming out of my prime," Jake blurted then he continued with, "toddy sounds good."

Now Jake always had a few doodads laying around left over from black ops. When you are black Ops, you don't exist so the equipment used doesn't exist either, so you can't turn that stuff in, if there's no record of you, or of you having equipment. There're always a Couple grenades nearby. With a holster mounted on the inside of the porch where he kept a judge. A five shot revolver that shoots long colt .45 and .410 shotgun shells. Jake doesn't kill Critters but sometimes he has to scare off a bear, or a wolf.

Jake's dad, use to say, "You have to share the land they were here first." When he was young with his dad they would camp, hunt and fish but only for food, never trophy. Living in Colorado and not have any antlers hanging on the barn or even in the house was very unusual, "Just because we had to kill for food, doesn't mean we show off the critters we throw on the grill."

So back to the porch and June brings out the hot rum toddies. The two of them sit and look at the stars. When Jake sees something strange in the sky.

"Do you see that," Jake asked.

June looked up from her phone and said, "What is that?"

Even their chocolate lab woke up and was staring up.

Written By
J.R. Wilson

The Adventures of
Jake & Archie

"What do you think, there Bullet," Jake asked, Bullet just whined a little then laid back down. What they were seeing looked like a couple satellites, that orbit the earth. But they weren't orbiting it appears like they were shooting at each other. In moments one was streaking down towards earth off to Jake and June's left. One started breaking apart and burned up coming down. It was off to their right. Jake and June sipped their hot rum toddies and just looked at each other in bewilderment. Jaws hanging open because in the blink of an eye these green beams came down to earth, four of them two on the left and two on the right were shining down to the ground from very high up.

"What the heck is going on?" June whispered to Jake.

"I don't know but I think we're about to find out," said Jake.

Coming up from the left side of the house were two odd little fellows, they looked like some kind of warrior. They were gray and green with odd-looking noses, small mouths and ears, a big head, they were about four and a half feet tall. Carrying what looked like rifles they started yelling some gibberish. Jake looked at them and replied, "You speak English on this ranch, you're not from around here. You're not local boys."

The two of them started messing with something on their chest and they started to speak English, "We are going to conquer this planet, you will be our slaves."

June hollered at them, "There's about seven billion folks on this planet. I figure they will have something to say about that!"

That very second the more belligerent alien raised his weapon, fired it and blew up Jake's pickup. It turned it to dust.

Jake yelled, "Hey you blew up my pickup! What the hell you little bastard," Jake told June to go in the house. He grabbed

Written By
J.R. Wilson

9

his judge and started firing. He hit them both with long colt .45s. Thinking it was over… but it wasn't the two of them got up a little worse for wear, and a green light came down.

"We will be back," they hollered, as they stepped into the beam. Jake grabbed a grenade and threw it into the beam.

He yelled back, "Here's a little something you can take with you," and when the beam went up with the two aliens, the grenade followed. June and Jake were looking up and saw a little flash of light. Then they could see a large ship heading off into space when it was almost out of sight, the sky lit up. It looked like the death star blowing up two rings came off it.

"What an amazing sight," a voice said while Jake and June just looked at each other.

"Who said that?" asked June. While they were staring at the sky they failed to notice two more aliens, but these two were different, these two were green and very clean. Their heads were big, but the features were more fitting to the head, ears were bigger, mouth was bigger than the others.

"So are we going to have a problem," Jake inquired.

"Oh… oh no! Not from us. You destroyed our enemies ship," The alien said.

June notice one of them was hurt so she took him into the house to tend to his arm and leg. The commander of the two is left with Jake. He asked if Jake could run out to the bushes and he dropped the survival bag. They really need it, to fix his partner up. Jake found the bag and brought it to the commander.

With the bag in hand the commander works on his navigator using a glowing rod he pulled from the bag. He hovers it over the wounded area and it is healed at a miraculous pace. While the navigator rests the commander and Jake sit out on the porch talking.

Written By
J.R. Wilson

The Adventures of
Jake & Archie

"Commander, I must ask, how is it you talk so American? Talking with you I feel like I'm talking to my neighbor," Jake queried,

"We have been watching you for thousands of years," the commander replied, "This is the first time in one hundred years I have been back. Last time I was here you were very primitive. Killing each other, waring with spears and bows and arrows. You didn't interest us, too primitive," replied the commander, "There are other beings that came here for experiments on your people. They are trouble. They make us all look bad" once the commander started talking... you couldn't get him to stop, "We have been monitoring your television from our planet I really like your shows, and the music," he laughed.

"So, you knew we had advanced over the years," replied Jake a little confused. "Why didn't you come back," Jake asked.

"Like I said, we weren't interested in your planet. It just kept us entertained, good shows," the commander reconfirmed, "Now we are in your dept for taking out that mother ship," the commander turned serious, "But I'm afraid they will be back."

"Who are those guys. They seemed like jackass's," Jake asked. He was still pissed about his truck.

"We created them to defend our planet," the commander explained, "They started out great. Then they conquered a planet that was attacking us, over and over again. When they took the planet, they wouldn't let our government come there and run things. As time passed, they drained the planet dry. They are warriors. They don't know about manufacturing, farming, or ranching. Just consume and conquer. Lately their attention has been on our planet. Now... probably yours to."

Jake came back with "Well... I have a few more grenades so we can take 'em," They both laughed.

Written By
J.R. Wilson

The Adventures of
Jake & Archie

"That no good Gruller. I chased him across three galaxies. We slipped from one galaxy to another shooting back and forth at each other," the commander explained, "When we got over your planet that's when we hit each other. My ship got the worst but both ships crashed. Oh… and we are sorry about your truck. Those guys can be… out of control. That was very creative when you tossed the grenade in the beam. Why didn't we think of that," the commander asked in a more commentative fashion, "What made you think to do that?"

"I was pissed, and they weren't getting away that easy. I just reacted that's all," replied Jake, "I had no intention of blowing up their ship I was just wanting to knock out their transporter or mater transference or whatever you guys called it."

While they were talking the commander's mother ship was in position to beam them up. So, the commander helped his navigator towards the beam just before they stepped in the commander turns and looks at Jake and says, "No grenades this time," and smiled.

Jake reassured him, "No grenades," and he smiled with a chuckle under his breath. Jake and June were now sitting back on the porch drinking their hot rum toddies they turned and looked at each other and at the same time they both said.

"Did that just happen," Jake said.

"I saw aliens," June said.

"Good so did I," said Jake.

They finished their toddies and went to bed.

Written By
J.R. Wilson

Chapter 2
The Car

It's the next morning and Jake is on the Porch standing and taking in the morning June approaches and hands him a coffee, "What a gorgeous morning" June observed.

"Thank you, I need some caffeine after last night," Jake replied.

"Did that really happen or was I dreaming," June asked afraid of the answer.

"Well… if you saw aliens then it wasn't a dream sweety," Jake reassured her.

They stood quietly sipping their coffee and looking out over their property. The ranch was at one time a large cattle producer eleven thousand five hundred acres with a two-thousand-acre lake that's about fifty yards from the house. The house is a large forty by eighty feet with a covered deck that wraps around the house. It was built sixty years ago but was completely refurbished and upgraded about five years ago. Some custom upgrades were added because of Jake's background in Black ops. Safety measures were required.

A new barnlike structure was added at the same time. It looks like a nice new barn but it's really a custom-built home. Inside there's a big open area with a bar and bedrooms along the side. A flow through fireplace in the center, two couches, a big screen TV, pool table, a shuffleboard table, a snooker table, and a poker table. This is a place for them to relax, play, drink, and watch games. There are, however, some secret rooms and a large basement. There's a pop up in the center of the roof with a .50 caliber sniper rifle sighted by remote camera. It also raises up to a second level under the rifle which has a mini chain gun also sighted by remote camera. When lowered, it just looks like a normal roof.

Rusty is one of the three from Jake's squad who designed it. He is a guru when it comes to gun smithing or machinist designs Rusty is the guy. This is not a typical ranch. Rusty is educated but loves fighting. Six-foot two blonde hair but balding a bit. He has a very good sense of humor according to Casey and Tech.

Jake sees a pickup coming up the driveway.

"Oh Jake, the fellas are back from their night on the town," June remarks, "Best get some breakfast cooking. They will be hungry," June continued as she headed back in the house.

Jake couldn't help wondering was last night's excitement over or was there more to come.

"Hey boss, what happened here where's your truck," inquired Tech.

"Aliens," Jake answered. The guys were coming up on the porch and they looked at each other.

Casey whispered to Tech and Rusty, "Damn Canadians," they both acknowledged. Cassey with a look. Casey was second in command when they all served together. He is an Expert marksman, as they all were, and a hand-to-hand combat instructor. Tech is primarily a demolition expert but is a computer whiz and a very good hacker. He stands about six foot and is a little stocky. Always ready to get into some action. He worships Jake, as Casey and Rusty do, they trust him with their lives, and he has saved them on more than one occasion.

So… the guys were hungry everyone sat down to eat. After breakfast, the guys started on their chores. Since cutting back on the number of cattle the ranch was self-reliant chickens

The Adventures of
Jake & Archie

a few hogs, about one hundred head of white faces cattle down from the usual eight or nine hundred head that Jake's dad ran every year. Jake wasn't wanting to handle so much. It was enough for profit and winter's food. Ranch was paid for. There's money in the bank. Jake just wanted to upgrade things, his buddies helped, wanting to leave their two sons a nice place.

Everyone was tired from a long day, after dinner Jake and his buds were sitting on the porch having a beer, "Boss so what aliens destroyed your truck. Was it Canadians, Europeans, Mexicans," asked Casey, "We can find these guys and make them pay!"

"I have no idea where they're from or who they are. It might be a tough nut to crack," Jake spoke under his breath almost in a whisper.

Rusty suggested they go shoot some pool. Casey, Tech and Rusty headed out to the Barn. Jake sat there wondering how the heck he could explain this to his insurance company defiantly a total loss.

The sun was setting a beautiful sunset Colorado Sunsets are indescribable. The guys were in the barn about half lit up from drinking beers and the occasional shots of tequila. Jake and June were on the porch talking when a green light, lit up the front yard and there stood the commander.

Jake says "Your back? I figured you were gone. What brings you back here?"

"Well, we wanted to do something for you after getting your truck destroyed," replied the commander, "So we have this gift for you." Jake looked a little puzzled. A portal opens up, a

Written By
J.R. Wilson

15

line in the air that spread apart and formed a rectangle and through it came a black car.

To Jake's surprise he said, "Hey, a Maserati Ghibli where did you get that?"

"Well, it looks like a Ghibli. We copied the Ghibli. Its aerodynamics was what we liked but believe me it's not a typical car. It has a hundred plus extras you won't find on this planet," the commander chuckled under his breath, "Now you need to check it out," he went on to say, "Lay your hand anywhere on the car." So, Jake did as he was asked and felt a tingle in his hand, it just surprised Jake. "Okay, you're good to go. Oh… you might want to sit in it and meet the car. It will teach you and fill you in on the features," the commander seemed rushed, "Bye now, got to go," and with that the green light appears, and the commander look back at Jake and said, "No grenades, okay?"

Jake laughed said, "I'll never use grenades on folks that give me a car. Only on those who destroy my pickup," He laughed. The commander beamed up. Once Jake laid his hand on the car, they became linked, of course Jake didn't know that… yet.

So, the guys returned from the Barn and noticed the car. Jake and June were sitting on the porch.

"Where did you get the car boss," asked Casey.

Jake replied, "Aliens."

"Wow… generous Canadians," Tech replied.

"Yep," says Jake, "Generous Canadians," he didn't want to or didn't know how to explain what happened without sounding nuts. So, they all walked around the car, looking it

Written By
J.R. Wilson

over. Jake opened the driver's door and sat down. A voice came from the dash.

"Welcome aboard Jake, glad to meet you."

Jake freaked, "What the... who said that?"

The door was closed so no one outside could hear what was being said, "I'm your car."

"You are a talking car well isn't that nice, what do I call you," asked Jake.

"I guess the car," replied the voice.

"No, that's stupid. Let's see... I think I will call you Jasper. No wait! Archie, you sound like an Archie, is that okay with you. Because that's what I'm calling you," said Jake.

"That's fine, I kind of like that name," the voice replied, "So Archie it is."

"I guess, you must be, kind of a driver asst or AI. I don't need driver assistance I can drive anything with wheels or tracks so you can just keep me company while we run around," Instructed Jake.

Okay if that's all you want. Fine but I'm more 'I' than 'A' there's nothing artificial about me. I'm a prototype... the only one. I was created for you last night. I am perfectly capable of driving without you Jake I'm a great driver."

"Okay," says Jake, "So you been in existence for... what? Forty-eight hours at most? I've been driving since I was twelve. Hmmm... who do you think has more time behind the wheel?"

"Good point Jake," answered Archie, "My programing of hundreds of drivers, mostly what you call racing drivers from NASCAR and Formula1."

"That's great. If we ever run up on a race track you can have a ball," Jake answered with a little smirk, "So tell me what you are supposed to teach me Archie?" Jake was being sarcastic,

The Adventures of
Jake & Archie

"So how about tomorrow we take a ride into town. I need to go to the store," Jake got out of the car and headed into the house with June and the guys.

"When are we taking her out for a little ride," ask Rusty.

"Oh… tomorrow we are going to town got to hit the grocery," replied Jake, "But I'm going alone. We will have plenty of time to take a road trip later. I need to get to know this car."

They all look at each other, "Get to know the car. Wow I don't believe I ever heard that before. What… You taking her to lunch," asked Rusty.

June was a little concerned, but she knew how the car got there, and it wasn't Canadians.

"Oh… and the car is a 'he' not a 'she' and his name is Archie okay," Jake said, a little on edge.

The guys could tell he wasn't his usual mellow self.

Written By
J.R. Wilson

Chapter 3
Test Drive

The next morning Jake walks out to car sitting out front. He realizes that maybe the barn is the best place to keep Archie. Jake climbs into the driver's seat and is greeted by Archie.

"Good morning Jake looks like a nice day," said Archie.

"And a good morning to you Archie. Shall we head to the store," asked Jake, "How do I start you up?" The motor starts all by itself with a very healthy sound. Deep and choppy like something off a drag strip, "Wow you have some power. Wonderful we should have some fun," Jake stated very impressed.

They head down the driveway and pull out on the county road. Jake gives it some throttle and is thrown back in his seat. With a big smile he said, "You are awesome let's see what you can do?"

Archie replied, "With pleasure sir."

The next thing that happens blows Jake's mind. He looks down at the speedometer and shows two hundred miles per hour. Jake lets off the throttle to slow down.

Archie says, "I thought you wanted to see what we could do?"

Jake replies "Two hundred is fast. Any faster and we would be traveling through time. I'm not ready for that."

Archie instructs Jake, "Hit the green button on the dash."

"Green button? What's the green button do," asks Jake.

"Just turn on the green button," Archie insisted.

"Why," Jake was teasing, "What's your obsession with the green button?"

Written By
J.R. Wilson

"Okay… I will explain," Archie replied in a louder volume then normal, "The button turns on an inertia suppressor or dampener. Whatever you want to call it. It turns off inertia."

"What," replied Jake. The statement wasn't something that Jake thought possible, "That's impossible you can't control inertia. Physics say it's impossible."

"Maybe for earthlings… but not for us. Now hit the damn button!"

Jake reaches over and slowing pushes the button, "You seem a little upset Archie. I didn't know you could get mad."

"You would make anybody mad. How do I teach you if you're going to buck me at every turn!"

"Sorry I didn't know you were so sensitive," Jake apologized. When he hit the button, everything changed and there was no pressure. Nothing, it was like sitting in his living room while the car zoomed on. Jake couldn't feel the turns or slowing or speeding up, nothing.

"This is your lesson for today. We will work on more tomorrow," Archie wasn't a teacher and had no tolerance. Jake was frustrated that he wanted to learn it all now, not piece meal little bits at a time. As they pulled up the driveway, Bullet came running out and when he saw the car he just stopped. No barking he just looked as if he didn't believe what he was seeing. Dogs sense things and Bullet realized this isn't a normal car. It's alive and he could sense that. But it wasn't a threat. Of course, Archie wasn't used to dogs, so he told Jake he has a nice dog. He is smart enough to tell the car was an intelligent being. Something Jake is still figuring out.

The Adventures of
Jake & Archie

Meanwhile in the little town twenty minutes down the road from the ranch. There were four Russians picking on a sixteen-year boy with autism. They were neighbors.

In a heavy Russian accent, "Oh… poor little man who only has part of his mind working," laughed the Russian the other three laughed with him. The boy's name is Joey. He was a nice boy, always wanting to help. He just couldn't understand why these strange foreigners were picking at him.

He goes into his house and talks to his mom. Joey is very upset, and his mom tries to comfort him but to no avail. He runs off to his room. While in his room Joey's window was open and at side of their house where he could hear the neighbors. The Russians were talking, and Joey realizes they are going to the store, but they don't shop locally because they didn't want folks to know they are living there. They drive thirty minutes to the large city up the highway nobody notices them there.

When they leave Joey goes around to their backdoor and sneaks in. Once inside he sees guns and explosives. One gun stands out. It's a double action .50 revolver, so he grabs it and goes out the front door.

Jake decides he needs to go to town because he didn't make it to the store on his test drive. He figures it's a good time to get June and Archie acquainted.

"Say June want to go for cruise into town, check out the car and go to the store."

June replies, "Sure sounds good, I have a list."
June remarks, "You know we have our picnic camp out in two days, so we need lots of hamburger and hot dogs, buns, chips I got it all listed."

Written By
J.R. Wilson

21

The Adventures of
Jake & Archie

"Okay Hun," Jake responds while taking a turn into town going the back way, old habits. As they cruise down a street of a subdivision, they both see a familiar face.

"That's Joey. What's he doing," observed June.

"Yeah! He's got a gun," said Jake, "Pull over Archie I need to check this out," Jake was a little nervous but more for Joey than himself.

As he gets out of the car, Archie says, "I will deploy a protective shield around you, so you don't get... ya know... shot."

"You can do that?" Asked a surprised Jake, "That's a handy jewel of a tip you could have let me in on a little sooner. We will talk later about this." Jake was wondering as he approached Joey, where did he get that dirty Harry-looking revolver, "Hi Joey! How ya doing bud," Jake is trying to be as friendly and nice as he could. But that's not Jake's strong point. So, this took a lot of effort.

"Hi Jake look what I have," Joey pointing the weapon towards the sky waving it around. Jake kept approaching and talking.

"Yeah, that's a nice-looking gun can I see it?" Jake asked cautiously. Joey wasn't sure if that was a good idea, but he liked Jake, because he and June were always nice to Joey. They always invited him and his mom to the picnic camp out.

"Well... I like it... So... you're my friend and I guess it's okay. I like to share," Joey said.

While this was going on three sheriff cars pulled up, just watching Jake. They know Jake. The whole for, which was a force of four including the sheriff, they're all former special forces, and Jake is the reason they live and work here. So, Joey hands Jake the pistol. As soon as he had the gun, Jake popped open the cylinder and the five shells fell into his hand. Jake

Written By
J.R. Wilson

holds his hand behind his back and opens it, so the deputies and the sheriff can see Jake unloaded the gun.

Jake slips the shells into his pocket when the deputies start to move. Jake gives them a subtle hand signal to stay back, "So this is a sweet gun where did you get it Joey," Jake was doing what he does best, dealing with the trouble. Joey seemed a little afraid to tell, but Jake reassured Joey it was all right. The sheriff isn't going to touch him.

Joey pointed to the house next door to him and bowed his head and spoke. "The four men that live there are mean to me. They went to the store in the city. So... I went through their back door and saw all these guns I figure they owe me for being mean to me. I took the pretty one, is that okay?"

"Joey that makes sense to me you're a good boy. How long have they lived here?" Jake asked.

"Two and a half weeks exactly," Joey answered confidently. Jake signaled the deputies to check out the house.

"Do you guys know of anyone new in town?" Jake asked the deputies. Their response was generally no. When the deputies saw weapons, handguns, rifles, handheld rocket launchers, and about five rockets, lots of explosives.

"Hey Joey, do you know what kind of car they drive?" asked one of the deputies.

Joey was positive, "It's a pretty, blue Cadillac. They park in back."

"Okay, so they come in the ally and park behind the house okay... great," Jake was thinking out loud.

"Men let's set up in the house and wait for them to come in. Joey, you need to go home and make sure you and your mom are safe. Go to her room it's on the far side of the house away from all this. Okay," Jake was giving orders. Joey agreed and ran home to tell his mom. The deputies were freaking out about all the weapons and explosives in the house. Jake filled in the sheriff on what Joey said. The deputies emptied the house into their cars. Automatic weapons, C4 explosives, and the rocket launchers filled three trunks. Then they moved their cars down the street and waited in the house.

After about thirty minutes of waiting a Caddy pulled in the back. They sit there and don't get out. The Russians know something is wrong.

The driver says speaking Russian, "Our marker is gone. Someone has opened the back door."

The officers and Jake are inside waiting and watching, "They know somethings up," whispered Jake to the sheriff. At that moment, the Caddy hit reverse and banged off things like a couple trash cans, and the side of the garage. They go flying down that alley still banging off stuff and they weren't even backing up anymore.

All this time June is still in the car talking with Archie who was curious, "How does Jake help the town? I know what Jake and the ranch are worth, it's substantial, but to keep a town going that will break him in a few years and you been doing this for five years?"

June said to Archie, "Did you check the town bank accounts?"

After a few seconds Archie said, "Oh my! Theres fifteen million in the town bank account isn't that a lot for a small town?"

June smiled and spoke, "Let me tell you a quick story."

"Almost five years ago Jake, Casey, Tech, and Rusty were sitting at the ranch trying to think of something that will make money for the town. They had only been out of the service for a few weeks."

"What about a food truck or two, those things make money" Rusty offered.

"No, we can't throw competition at our diners and fast-food restaurants. We wouldn't make head way," replied Tech, he went on to say, "The income must come from outside sources. There's not enough money in town."

They all knew Tech was right, the room got quiet. Jake was exceptionally quiet. Then Jake smiled like he had something sinister in mind, "Do you guys remember the Sheik? We had to harass him for the government and how easy it was. We had access to everything including security."

"Yeah... so," said Casey.

"I remember he had a huge amount of gold and priceless art. We could have taken all we wanted if we weren't on the job. We aren't on the payroll anymore," Jake pointed it out.

"So, what are you saying Jake," Casey wondered.

Then Jake jumped up, "I say we go back and help ourselves to some goodies!"

"You must be crazy, he will never stop hunting us down," Tech warned.

"What if I said that will never be a problem," Jake was being reassuring to the men. Then he went into his whole plan. Anyway, they contact an old buddy with a cargo plane and next thing you know they're on their way. They land on a secret air strip they used when they were deployed in the desert while on active duty.

"Seems like we were just here," says Tech.

"We were just here about six weeks ago," Casey remarked.

The Adventures of
Jake & Archie

They did what they did so well and slipped in without anyone noticing. Loaded with everything from gold coins, gold bars, and some gold statues. They were back on the plane and on their way home in no time at all. The sheik never knew what happened. Jake called the Sheik from America and told him he had his stuff. He told the Sheik to bring two million in cash to America, and we will swap. They did as they were told, no guns no problem. Jake reasoned two million is lunch money for the Sheik. Gold and art were worth a lot more and some had been in his family forever. Jake knew he would pay, no doubt. So… about six months later Jake and the guys… they did it again! Same smooth exchange. The Sheik was beside himself.

He wanted to know why they were picking on him, and he knew he couldn't do anything about it. Jake looked at him and said, "We won't ever do this again if you agree to direct deposit five hundred thousand every month into our towns account. The Sheik jumped at that. He's worth about fifty billion so he could afford it.

"You should have just asked me I probably would have given you the money," stated the sheik.

"No, you wouldn't have given us a thing," Jake corrected the sheik.

"Yes. This is correct I wouldn't," laughed the Sheik.

So, he still pays. Jake's plan worked. Planning missions is what Jake did in special services, and he is good at it, always taking in the big picture. Now we run our town, take care of payroll for city workers, and help our schools without any help from the feds, which gives our students more opportunities to grow and learn. Without Government telling us what we can and can't do. There's always some left at the end of the month so that money goes into an interest-bearing account. It's the operating capital and emergency fund for our little town. That's why the

Written By
J.R. Wilson

large balance that money is spent carefully. So that's how it all started. Jake and the boys saved our little town. No one goes hungry. It all goes back into the community," June looked around and finished with, "At least I don't have to wait tables anymore. Well... except at the ranch," she laughed." You know the sheik comes here from time to time he likes to ski."

Jake comes running and jumps into Archie to chase down the four Russians. They bolt off. The sheriff was following close behind. It only took a minute or two before Archie was right on the Caddy's tail.

Jake said, "We must stop them, or run them off the road. We can't use the laser canon with the sheriff behind us it might freak him out."

Archie informs Jake, "We could use the EMP."

"Okay... What! EMP Dang-O! When were you going to tell me about that little tidbit?" Jake is fuming "Okay hit the EMP."

The Caddy starts slowing down Archie fried the circuits in it. When the car stopped all four doors opened and the Russians came out shooting. The sheriff pulled up next to Archie and he was returning fire with his shot gun. Bullets were bouncing off Archie and all Jake had was his judge, so he opened the door and stood up knowing Archie had protected him. The sheriff was screaming at him to take cover; Jake was standing behind the driver's door. He looked over at the sheriff and smiled then he turned his attention to the Caddy, he took aim quickly and he fired. That long colt .45s went through the caddy's doors like a hot knife through butter. Jake was accurate and soon all four Russians were on the ground three dead, and one critically wounded. June is sitting in Archie watching Jake.

Jake walks over to the wounded Russian, kneels down and grabs the wounded man by his shirt and pulls him up.

The Russian with a very heavy accent says, "How did you know?"

"What are you doing here," shouted Jake.

The Russian was getting weaker, "We miss you. More will come."

"Who will come and who sent you," Jake was pissed off and wanted to know what this was about.

"Vladimir sent us. There are many of us coming," the Russian was so weak it was just a whisper. Then he died. Jake just slams The Russian back down on the ground. June saw all of this, she was worried about Jake.

The sheriff was standing behind Jake. When Jake looked up he said, "Vladimir well that doesn't help. Hell, about every other Russian boy is named Vladimir."

The sheriff was calling the ambulance and tow truck. Then he looked at Jake, "Why did they stop, did their car break down because that is some awesomely bad luck for them."

"Yeah... bad luck. It doesn't matter, freaken Russians. You should radio your deputies to head to the ranch. You know these guys will hit the station first."

After being alerted the deputies were off to the ranch. Trunks of their cars are still full of goodies. The sheriff and Jake agreed that the sheriff station wasn't safe, if there were an assault they would hit the sheriff's office first to cover their backs. There was no trouble, while hitting the ranch, there wouldn't be any surprises, no law to worry about. Jake walks back to the car cell in hand calling Casey at the ranch.

"Yo," Casey answers the phone.

Written By
J.R. Wilson

The Adventures of
Jake & Archie

"Case, red alert! You guys get vested with plates I'm headed home. I'll fill you in," He climbs into the car and looks at June, "Are you okay honey? I know that had to be scary," Jake was concerned for her.

June smiled at him, "I'm fine," June says, "Archie reassured me, nothing in that Caddy could penetrate this car and if by some awful miracle and they win they would never get in this car. It was like watching a movie some shots bounced of the windshield I was thinking, Great 3D," June laughed nervously, "And by the way good shooting ole man."

Jake put his arm around her and said, "Should we go to the store? I called the guys gave them a heads up."

"Oh… yeah! The store," June yelped.

They swing by. Jake is worried. He wants to head straight home.

June says, "Wait here," and she runs in.

Jake is stunned, "Wait here? We need a lot of stuff and it's going to take both of us to get it done," Jake was about to get out when June came running back.

Once inside she said, "Ok let's go."

Jake looked at her as Archie pulled out of the parking lot, "What just happened? What did you do," Jake asked her with a curious look on his face.

June in a casual way said, "Oh, my sister was working. I gave her the list and my card, she will take care of getting everything. Probably more than everything and they deliver, so let's go."

Jake loves her problem solving. They started for home. Twenty minutes is a long time when you're headed home worried.

Archie breaks the quiet, "this might be a good time to bring up a feature."

Written By
J.R. Wilson

29

The Adventures of
Jake & Archie

Jake looks at the screen on the dash and says, "What You got in your bag of tricks for me?"

Archie says, "How about we fly home," and with that said, up they go. Very fast it throws June and Jake back in their seats.

"Wow," Says Jake, "A little warning… dang-O."

"Hit the green button," Archie reminds Jake. So that's what he does, and everything gets calm.

June asks, "What the hell is that button?"

Jake laughed, "It's a smooth ride button," Next thing they knew they were over their property.

"Maybe we should land on the road before we get to the gate and turn off the stealth. So, we don't freak everyone out. There's no traffic so it should be fine," Archie points out.

"Yeah… good idea… wait STEALTH!? We were invisible," Jake is really getting tired of this, "Stealth that's nice, no more surprises tonight, okay?"

"Fine, I thought you would be happy. Sorry I didn't know it would upset you," Archie remarked with bit of an attitude.

"Look I'm tired. It's been a hell of day. I got shot at. I shot folks, and the Russians have found my home… so I'm a little testy, okay!"

"Oh… Jake before you get out, this is for you," a little slide comes out from the dash on it is an ear pod, "Put that in your ear and we stay in touch with each other."

"What's the range," Jake asks.

Archie pointed out, "Don't know the range, because it's new like me," Archie was trying to lighten the mood.

"Thank you, Archie, this is the first thing that hasn't freaked me to out. Thank you again. You're a good egg Archie," Jake was trying to be sincere.

Written By
J.R. Wilson

The Adventures of
Jake & Archie

Written By
J.R. Wilson

Chapter 5
Home Coming

Jake and June were glad to be home, and it was in one piece, so nothing happened… yet. They went in the house and Archie parked himself in the barn. Back in the house Jake filled in the guys on what happened in town. They were a little taken aback and somewhat upset. They didn't get in on what they called fun. Jake started going over what the guys had been working on.

"Okay," Jake thought *Hmmm, I seem to be saying 'OK' a lot. Never noticed that before*, "Okay… Casey are we good for defensive action?"

"Yes sir," replied Casey, "We placed claymores, about forty, set around the perimeter of the house and barn just in case they get close. With sixty pipe bombs we buried in the tree line, I figure... Yes sir! I believe it, we're good to go. We have four tablets for fifty cameras and motion sensors. All detonation is hardwired so radio transmissions won't set them off. No trip wires, this is so we can control which ones need to be fired. The big screen in Rusty's workshop and the tablets will monitor cameras and motion sensors. all bombs can be fired from any touch screen," Casey finishes his report.

"Alright Casey sounds good. Everyone should stay here in the house tonight it is the safest place with all the improvements. We are bullet proof." Jake insisted, "So what do you say June how about making a batch of hot rum totties. We will be on the porch, come on guys."

Jake noticed a jeep coming up the road, using his tablet the cameras picked up the Jeep. They all watch the tablet. The jeep turned up the driveway.

"Are we expecting anyone," Jake wondered.

"No," Replied June, "Not that I know of."

Written By
J.R. Wilson

The Adventures of
Jake & Archie

"Hmmm… well stand ready men," Jake barked. The jeep pulls up and out steps Jake and Junes two sons.

"I'll be… It's the boys. June our sons are home!"

Jamie and Tony were glad to be home, the boys are big like their Pop over six foot and strong. Mom and Pops are relieved, everybody is okay. Lots of hugging going on mom dad, Casey, Tech, and Rusty everyone hugging on the porch.

"What brings you home. You both got leave at the same time, how did you manage that," Jake was happy but also curious.

"Well," Jamie said, "My commander called me in and told me that our intel picked up some communication. That Russians found you and were coming here."

Tony remarked a bit worried, "We were monitoring on our ship and picked up similar intel. I have accumulated about a month of leave. The captain told me to go home. He remembers you Pop and knew if Russians were rumored to be headed here it was probably a certainty. So… here I am."

"Great did you coordinated so you arrive together," Jake asked.

"Nope," said Tony, "We ran into each other at the Denver airport. Which is amazing, that airport is huge. How we met up was at the car rental. I heard that Denver airport is the biggest in the country it's supposed to be bigger than the city of San Francisco I don't know if that's true, but I believe it."

Jake laughed, "Well I'm glad you're here I missed you guys."

Jamie is a marine in Reckon and special forces, black ops, he joined about five years ago. Tony is the older of the two by a year and seven months. He joined the Navy and is a seal he's been in almost six years. Jake is proud of his boys, but it didn't stop him from worrying.

Written By
J.R. Wilson

Jake began to explain what's going on. The boys were wide eyed they couldn't believe it.

"Pops is getting more action retired than I am on duty," replied Tony laughed but a little envious to.

"We are expecting some trouble. We've been setting up a perimeter of mines and pipe bombs. Stay away from the trees we have mines everywhere," Jake said very seriously.

"Ok Pop, tell us what you want us what to do," Tony volunteered.

"Right now, we stay in the house we will see them coming. If they come on our land," Jake looked around at everyone, "If they do, they become fair game. Everyone gear up vests and extra plates fill up on ammo," Jake snapped out orders like he used to.

"Hey boss, we got movement east side along the back road," Shouted Tech, "Their coming through the trees," he continued.

"Ok let's take a look," using his tablet Jake had about eight cameras spread out about halfway into the trees Jake pushed the activation for the sector they were coming through, "Try this on for size, you Russian pricks," and with that he hit the fire button. Six pipe bombs go off with a bit bigger explosion than Jake thought it would be. Russian bodies and parts flying everywhere.

"Wow," said Jake, "That was a much bigger boom than I figured."

"That should have sent a message to those Russians," June remarked.

There are about eight of them left Jake grabs the PA systems mic, "Well it doesn't look too good for you now. We can blow up the rest of you. Or you walk out lay your weapons on the ground, don't drop them they might go off," Slowly they walked out, "Ok take off your belts, remove your coats, take off your boots, then pull up your pant legs," they responded to the instructions. Casey and Rusty found a couple of knives strapped to their ankles while frisking them. They chained them up in the clearing next to a tree, handcuffs, leg irons they weren't going anywhere. Tech was on the phone to their contact in D.C.

When he hung up, he told Jake, "Two chinooks are coming should be here anytime."

"Thanks… and good work Tech," Jake praised him.

Chapter 6   The Boys Meet Archie

Meantime Tony and Jamie head out to the barn. When they entered, they noticed Archie right away, "When did Pop get a Maserati… dang this is a nice car," said Tony. Archie hasn't said a word. The boys decided to sit inside where they could talk in peace.

"This is nice… man! It's like sitting in a Bentley with lots of power," remarked Jamie.

"Yeah… it's sweet." Tony agreed.

Jamie remembered, "When we left Denver airport and we saw all those black Suburban's at that hotel."

"Yeah, there was eight or so, we thought it was secret service for the President," Tony responded, "But you know those Russians might be staying there. If so, the boss is probably there also. What did Pop say… he thought the leaders name is Vladimir. If we could get our hands on him, it might end this crap."

"Copy that bro," said Tony.

"Good idea boys," Archie hollered out. The boys both jumped looking at each other.

Written By
J.R. Wilson   35

"Who said that," Tony looked a little worried. He was thinking the car was bugged.

Archie says, "It's me the car, Jake calls me Archie. I knew you were his sons when you touched me, your DNA told me so."

"What the hell you talking about? What are you A. I.," demanded Jamie.

"No, I'm just 'I'" Archie snapped back, "All I'm saying is we should go get this guy at least confirm they're staying there!"

"Sure, let's just drive up and storm the hotel all two of us. Great idea there Archie whose an 'I'…" Tony remarked sarcastically.

"Do me a favor hit the green button please." Ask Archie.

"That green button," Jamie was pointing.

"Please it's for your own good," stated Archie.

"What do you mean, our own good," said Tony, "What's the deal with the green button Archie?"

Archie made an angry face blowing his top on the dash screen. He yells, "Hit the damn button!"

So, Jamie hit the button, and it lights up green. Archie is thinking, *it must run in the family green button phobia.* Before the boys knew it the barn doors opened and they backed out. Archie goes stealth and shoots up into the sky, his navigation had them over Denver in minutes. They head east towards the airport.

Jamie hollers, "That's the Hotel."

Archie maneuvers around front and two black Suburban's were still there but the other four were gone. After the boys stopped freaking out, about a flying car and no inertia. This was a lot to take in, but they seemed to adjust.

Written By
J.R. Wilson

The Adventures of
Jake & Archie

Jamie says, "Set it down we need info, we need to know if they're staying here and if so what floor and room. I'll go in and have a look."

"Not alone... I'm going in with you," Tony demanded, "Ok set it down somewhere no one can see us come out of stealth."

"Copy that Jamie," Archie trying to sound military. Archie pulled up in front of the hotel; the boys get out like a customer getting a room. Yeah... a customer with a Glock and suppressor.

They stroll in, and a female voice calls out, "Jamie," Jamie looks around and over at Tony. Tony just shrugged then Jamie noticed a girl behind the reservations desk. He walks over.

"Connie is that you," she was so happy to see Jamie. Jamie introduced Tony.

"So, this is my brother Tony. Tony, this is Connie. We took drivers ed together in high school. She was awful at driving," he laughed.

Tony said, "Nice to meet you, Connie. Were you really a bad driver?"

Connie laughed and said, "I still am."

Tony whispered to Jamie, "We don't have time for this."

Jamie turned to Connie and asked, "Are there any Russians staying here?"

Connie moved in close and said, "They have the whole top floor."

"Really," Jamie wanted to sound amazed.

Connie continued, "Most of them just left, the head guy is still here and one of them, an older guy is in the bar."

Written By
J.R. Wilson

The Adventures of
Jake & Archie

Tony and Jamie just looked at each other and headed to the bar. Jamie ran back quickly to Connie and invited her to the picnic camp out.

She was excited, "I forgot about the picnic camp out. I haven't been to one in years."

Jamie said, "Great it's Saturday. Gotta go," he ran to join Tony.

"Got a date for Saturday," Jamie smiled they walked into the hotel bar and there was an overweight man sitting at the bar drinking Vodka.

The boys sat at a table. Tony got up and walked to the bar and ordered a couple beers. He hears the man on his cell talking with a heavy Russian accent. Tony grabbed the beers and went back to the table. Tony was Whispering to Jamie what he heard. Waiting to make their move, Tony says, "I'll stick my gun in his ribs and walk him to the room."

"Sounds like a plan" Jamie agreed.

At that moment, the Russian gets up and walks out toward the elevator. Tony and Jamie do the same. They gave each other a look like this will work too, just follow him up. In the elevator door closes and Jamie and Tony whip out their side arms. The Russian looked a little shocked at first, then he smiled.

In a heavy Russian accent, "You won't shoot me. I have the diplomatic immunity so you can't touch me," He started laughing. Tony smacked him upside the head using his gun hand and dropped the Russian.

"See we can touch you. It was real easy… want me to show you again," Tony asked.

The Russian put his hand up, "No more you, are in big trouble whoever you are."

Tony laughs "Oh… don't worry about me I'm going to be fine."

Written By
J.R. Wilson

38

The Adventures of
Jake & Archie

The door opens. The Russian gets up and the three of them head down the hall towards the suite. Vladimir is supposed to be in. They reach the door, and the Russian opens it, and the boys follow him in. Vladimir is in one of the two bedrooms. Jamie shoves the Russian to the floor face down.

"You stay there and don't move, and you might live through this," Jamie was very serious. The Russian knew he was going to die. He was thinking of how he could get out of there.

Tony checked the first room "Clear," he whispered to Jamie. He pointed to the other door. both him and Jamie moved to each side of the door. When they broke in, Vladimir took a shot at them, they both fired back.

"Dang it... I think we killed him," Jamie said.

"Wait," Tony was over Vladimir checking him for life, "He has on a vest on," Tony cuffed him. Before they could get out the other Russian was standing at the door with a gun. Jamie and Tony turned and saw him. Both Jamie and Tony returned fired at the same time. This Russian wasn't wearing a vest he was dead before he hit the floor.

Jamie said, "I warned him to lay there still if he wanted to live through this. I am not responsible for him, not following instructions. If he laid there he would still be breathing,"

Tony nodded, "Yep, his own fault."

When the three of them got to the lobby there was only a couple of folks walking by.

Jamie asked, "Tony take him to the car I need to stop at the desk I'll just be a minute."

"Copy that bro... Don't be long. We need to get home," Replied Tony excited, adrenalin will do that.

Jamie went over to Connie and told her, "Homeland Security and the feds will be showing up. None the Russians

Written By
J.R. Wilson

will be back. Close off the top floor don't let anyone up there it's a crime scene. Okay?"

Connie said, "What happened up there?"

"Oh… you know Russians… they don't listen. They should have followed our instructions, and they would be fine. Oh well." said Jamie.

"So… see you Saturday Jamie," Connie hoped.

"Looking forward to it Connie," Jamie replied walking out the door.

Chapter 7
Vladimir

Once they had Vladimir in the car they hog tied him, gagged him, and blind folded him. They even stuck plugs in his ear. Archie drove off and once they were out of sight of anyone. He took off, with stealth on and in minutes they were pulling back in the barn. They had been gone for a total of about forty-five minutes. So... no one missed them. When they walked Vladimir into the kitchen June was surprised.

"We have a guest," She remarked.

"Well not exactly mom but Pop should be happy," said Jamie.

When Jake walked in the kitchen and saw Vladimir, he didn't know who he was, "Who's this a surprise guest?"

Jamie laughed, "This is the big boss Vladimir."

"Really! What did you boys do," Jake asked a little upset.

"Well Pop," Jamie started to explain. About Seeing the black Suburban's and meeting Archie. When he finished Jake and June were a bit shocked. Jake sat there quietly for a few minutes. He stood up looking at his son's and he smiled.

"You know I forget how good you two are. You're men and good at your job. I forget to recognize that, you understand being my sons that I worry. Your mom worries... anyway we can't help that, your back and you have the villain. Good work we will discuss Archie later. Oh... yea what happened to their commander wasn't he with Vladimir?"

Jamie turned and said. In a calm and direct tone, "He died it was sudden."

Written By
J.R. Wilson

"Vladimir, you met my sons, you're lucky your still alive," said Jake.

"I am not a villain, and I have diplomatic immunity! You and your brats are going to be in big trouble," yelled Vladimir.

"Shut it," Jamie yelled like he's British or something.

"We know you came to blow up our little town and we know your men were going to attack our home. So as far as diplomatic immunity goes, huh you sneak into our country, you are terrorists by definition." Jake said, "Your own Country doesn't want you back. Apparently, you are part of the Russian mafia. See this isn't about country verses country you attack my ranch. You try to kill my family. This ranch is my world when you step on my property, you're in my world I am in charge no lawyers or judges. If I have my way you won't see tomorrow," Jake was getting hostile, "I know what your plan was blow up some buildings in our town. A diversion so everyone will be busy in town and then you attack our ranch." Jake continues, "It was a decent plan except it was executed by Morons, it might have worked if we hadn't squashed it like a bug."

Jake, the boys, Tech, Casey and Rusty were talking. The deputies went back to town, the sheriff stayed behind and was standing by the kitchen door listening.

Jake started, "You guys know, and I hate to say it in front of my boys, but I want that Russian piece of crap dead he tried to invade our ranch! Humm why? Get him in here I want to talk to him."

Vladimir says, "You don't remember me do you."

Jake replying "No... should I?"

"About fifteen years ago you killed my brother and my son," Vladimir tells him.

"About fifteen years ago..." Jake was thinking out loud, "Yeah, I remember Yugoslavia. We got in a fire fight, I do

Written By
J.R. Wilson

42

remember you, you got wounded! Your right, I did put them down and it wasn't easy you guys had a sniper keeping us busy. So that's why your here revenge?"

"No," replied Vladimir, "Not revenge... Vengeance!"

"Doesn't seem to be working out for you does it. When you traffic in young girls, you're nothing but scum. Let's see we brought back around ten girls to America on that mission and yeah, I personally took out your brother and son, and I would do it again in a New York minute. Someone should tell these kids Spring Break isn't what you imagine. These traffickers hang out at spring break resorts they drug 'em and take 'em," Jake warned.

Jake gathers his family to talk some more, "I really don't want to put him on the helicopter. He's right... he has diplomatic immunity. They will set him free. It just depends on who takes custody of him. I really want to put a couple rounds in him."

"I know Pops, but you can't. I can't... now if he was shooting at us then that's different," Jamie said excited. Then they hear a shot then another.

"What the hell is going on now Jake," June asked.

"Don't know," responded Jake. They all walk outside and see the sheriff standing over Vladimir. Sheriff looked over at Jake.

"Strangest thing... that Russian tried to escape. He came at me, and my reflexes took over, and I plugged him," reported the sheriff.

"Well... Okay...okay, that's fine," said Jamie nervously, "What do you think Dad,"

"He wasn't with the other prisoners so no witnesses. All I can say is we are glad you didn't get hurt sheriff," Jake said, "I say throw him in a body bag let the spooks figure all this out. Helicopters should be here soon. I think I can hear them now."

Written By
J.R. Wilson

The Adventures of
Jake & Archie

After loading the body bags on one helicopter and the prisoners on the other, it was kicking back time with a hot rum toddy, time. Jake, his sons, Casey, Tech, and Rusty were all sitting on the porch sipping hot rum toddies. when a green light shined in the house.

"Not again now what do they want," Jake complained.

"Who… Who is 'they'," Tony wondered.

"I think… you're going to find out," Jake responds and then a green light shined down if the front yard and one of those nasty Grullers beamed down.

"What do you want now," Jake asked a little put out after the day they had.

The alien said, "Want? We have what we want, we beamed your wife on board. We know it was you that destroyed our Mothership."

"How do you know that? If I destroyed your mothership, how did you find out," Jake snapped back, "You took my wife?"

"Yes. We have her. The mothership you blew up transmitted a message and video before it blew, it was some sort of chain reaction. So now you must pay," threatened the Gruller.

"You have my wife up there," when Jake finally looked over at the guys, they were just sitting jaws hanging down eyes all bugged out, "Hey! Snap out of it, you guys! Dang guys… you never seen an alien before?"

"NO," they said it together as if they rehearsed it.

"Okay… they took your mom boys, my wife," Jake was trying not to laugh but all the guys broke out laughing. Jake says, "I got twenty says she's back in under ten minutes."

Laughing Casey says, "An hour."

Tech, "Twenty-four hours."

Rusty, "two hours."

Written By
J.R. Wilson

The Adventures of
Jake & Archie

That nasty Gruller is talking away about all the stuff their going to do to June. While he was talking the green light reappears and then it vanished. June comes out the front door.

"Do you have any idea what happened to me," June hollered, "Here take this," She handed Jake one of their what appears to be a rifle, "Well those little bastards will think twice before they beam me up again. I took the gun from one of them. Then I started shooting it, not intentional it just kept going off, so they beamed me back. I need a toddy!" June walks in the house.

"Under ten minutes guys," Jake holds out his hand. Casey and Tech paid up. Rusty said he left his money in their house out back. He always leaves his money somewhere other than his pocket.

"Hey June, why did the gun keep firing," Jake asked nicely.

June stuck her head out the door, smiled and said, "Cause, I kept pulling the trigger."

When the alien or Gruller received a message saying they beamed her back he didn't know things had gone wrong in the ship. He stood there for a minute or two just staring, not knowing what to say. The green light appears he walks to it, "We will be back to conquer your world!"

"Sure, you will… you ugly little pug. Here take this with you," and Jake throws another grenade into the beam and up went one Gruller and one grenade.

Jake and June started to laugh. Jake said, "Twice! I've done it to them twice! These guys are about as sharp as a soggy sponge," Jake remarked hardly able to contain himself. June was in tears laughing so hard. The guys were wondering what's so funny, then the ship blew up. It was hardly out of our

Written By
J.R. Wilson

atmosphere, "Good thing it was smaller ship," Jake pointed out. Then the green light appeared and there stood the commander.

Jake greeted him, "Hey commander what's up."

The guys on the Porch went back to bug eyed jaws hanging down.

"So…" the commander said, "You did it again," he even chuckled, "Grullers are on their way here. Be ready, use the car. You have about twenty-four hours before they reach your moon. Goodbye for now, see you soon. We will be back to help you."

"Great, thanks for the heads up," Jake said grateful.

So his sons and the crew were looking at Jake, "So when you said alien… it wasn't Canadians… or Mexicans… or Cubans, you meant," and Casey pointed up. Jake smiled and nodded.

"You guys kept saying Canadians and what not, all I ever said was aliens," said Jake with a smile.

Chapter 8
Gruller's Fleet

Jake went out to the barn to have a talk with Archie, "Hey there Archie doing okay," Jake was trying to catch Archie off guard.

"Well Jake, you did it again didn't you," Jake sat down in front of the car.

"Yep, looks that way, I didn't mean to blow up that first ship I just wanted to knock out their transporter so they couldn't come back down. The ship blowing was a bonus."

"What about the one tonight," Archie queried.

"Oh… I meant to blow that sucker up. These guys are starting to get on my nerves! They took my wife, so I had to make sure they don't try that again," Jake was upset and wanted Archie to go out and meet the Gruller fleet headed to earth. He was having trouble asking Archie.

"Okay… what about the fleet coming this way are we going to head them off," asked Archie. Jake was surprised Archie knew he would agree.

"Let's do this thing," Jake responded, "I didn't know you knew but I guess I should have expected as much."

Written By
J.R. Wilson   47

The Adventures of
Jake & Archie

Once they were off, Archie was filling in Jake on ways to attack. Jake hit the green button and Archie and Jake shot out of the atmosphere like a bullet.

"Okay, Jake stuff you should know," Archie directed Jake to watch the screen, "These are nanites, they make up every part of this car from tires to the roof, everything. They are alive and will let you know if you do something they don't like," Archie continued, "They keep the car repaired or modify it to create things like the EMP. The power plant is in the floor it is about 8 inches thick and covers the whole floorboard. what does that say to you?"

"Try not to expose the floor to any enemy," Jake blurted.

"Very good Jake. That plant could power a city indefinitely. Any questions Jake?"

"Only about a hundred, but I'll start with one, are you indestructible," asked Jake.

"In most cases yes, but if my power plant gets corrupted or penetrated the whole car me, will turn to dust," said Archie in a matter-of-fact manor.

"So that's it End of days, game over," Jake replied.

"The nanites are dependent on the power plant. In the first hour they can be revived, but after an hour game over," Archie informed Jake.

"How do I revive you," Jake wondered out loud.

"A huge amount of electricity, not quit a lightning strike," replied Archie.

Jake went on to say, "I was thinking... do we have a chance to win?"

"Fifty-fifty," Archie quickly replied, "Just kidding we can do this."

Jake was amazed. A computer with a sense of humor and also how fast they were going. In a joking way Jake said,

Written By
J.R. Wilson

The Adventures of
Jake & Archie

"Archie are you able to time travel," Jake chuckled. He was kidding. But Archie wasn't answering in about an hour they were past the moon. Jake couldn't believe where he was.

"Hey Archie," but Jake was interrupted.

"We are getting a call," Archie announced.

"Who is it Archie?"

"It's the commander. Should I put him through?"

"Of course," Jake replied. The commander came through in video on the dash screen, "Hey commander, what's up? We are on our way."

Commander asked, "Have you engaged the fleet?"

"Not yet, I think we might have a plan," Jake went on.

"Can you guys take on the fighters and we will do the rest," asked Jake.

"Ok, Jake good hunting," replied the commander.

"Plan, what plan Jake," Archie wondered.

"Can we penetrate the mothership if we get up a head of steam. That is if the Nanites think they can handle it. Is there a way to check with them?" Jake asked.

"Jake I'm always in contact with the nanites. They say they can reinforce the skin and seal up the wheel wells." Archie informed Jake. 'No problem, Jake' Was spelled out on the dash screen. Archie laughed, "They're talking to you Jake."

"Ok where's the fleet," Jake asked.

"We wait here, and they will be on us in about eighteen mins," Archie answered.

"Is the stealth engaged?" Jake inquired.

"Oh yeah… we are prepared," Archie reassured Jake, "Eighteen minutes feels like eighteen hours," Archie mumbled.

Jake laughed, "Yeah… waiting to battle can feel that way… but it won't be long then we kick butt, and we do it fast. Move like lighting, hit 'em fast hit hard then do it again. Here

Written By
J.R. Wilson

they come, are you ready Archie? You ready nanites?" The dash screen lit up 'Go! Go! Go!'

Archie says, "Let's get 'em!"

Chuckling Jake took control and circled around then climbed up above the first Mothership. He then aimed the front of Archie straight down, "Ok punch it," with that they went right to light speed and blew through that ship, so quick Jake blinked, and they were below the ship.

"What was that? Our ship is out of commission," Gruller captain yelled.

"Captain there's a big hole going right through our ship, our engines are dead and there are fires everywhere," The first officer reported.

"Okay, it worked once let's do it again Archie," Jake ordered.

"Okay Jake should we do the same maneuver," Archie asked, "if so, may I do it?"

"Sure, why not," replied Jake, "Have at it."

It's a good thing the green button is on. When Archie started the maneuver, it was done so fast it would have squished Jake, if the button was off. Zip zap and they blew right through the next mothership Jake sat back and looked around as they went through the mothership even though they went through at super speed.

Jake thought he saw… "Is that a food court. You guys have food courts," Jake was wondering what they eat.

Archie replied, "Sure, all civilizations have food courts you didn't think it was just an earth thing, did ya?"

Jake looked at the screen, "I really never thought about it. Huh… food courts. Live and learn," Jake was musing.

"Can we get out of here now," Jake was tired.

Written By
J.R. Wilson

The Adventures of
Jake & Archie

"Heads up two fighters right in front of us Jake," Archie called out.

"Well let's take 'em out," Jake yelled. Both laser canons light up and eliminated them, "Where's the commander?"

"Right here Jake, we got this. Great job you two," the commander signaled.

"We are outta here," Jake called back, "We have a picnic to set up tomorrow." Jake was thinking out loud. On the ride back.

Jake asks Archie, "So what exactly is this fazing you mentioned," Archie was quiet again, "Look Archie this is the second time I asked you a question and you clam up. Are you going to teach me all this stuff or not," Jake was miffed.

"This is advanced stuff you're asking and there's so much you need to learn first," Archie explained.

"That's bull… just answer my questions," Jake snapped.

"Okay… Alright… Jake when you climb a ladder do you just jump from the bottom step right to the top step," Archie asked.

"Of course not," responded Jake.

"It's the same thing you must go one step at a time. We can't jump ahead. A lot of what you're learning now has to become second nature to you, and that takes time. Then we move on to other things," assured Archie.

Jake knows he's right he made the same speech to recruits, "Okay, you made your point," Jake said softly, "But can you answer me this one question. Can we time travel?"

"All right, I will do this one. The answer is, no… not at this time," Archie answered.

"WHAT!? What the hell kind of answer is that?" Jake Barked.

Written By
J.R. Wilson

The Adventures of
Jake & Archie

Archie started to laugh, "It's the only one you're going to get. Ask me again in a couple months," Jake didn't respond. The earth was getting closer, "Ten mins till we land." Archie announced.

"This is The National Aeronautics Space Administration does anyone copy out beyond the moon," Archie asks, "Jake do we respond?"

"Sure. why not they can't see us," replied Jake.

"Well…" said Archie, "Even if we aren't stealth, they can't see us, they can't photo us, they can't see us on radar."

"No photos. Really," Jake questioned, "Yeah give me a mic I'll talk to them."

"You don't need a mic, just talk," Archie instructed.

"Hello NASA, what can I do for you," Jake called out.

"Yes, this is National Aeronautics Space Administration who are we talking to?"

"Look you guys called me, and NASA is good enough. We're about to land you don't have to spit out your whole name okay," Jake chuckled.

"We were tracking a fleet coming this way," Nasa came back.

"Oh yeah… well… they aren't going to make it. They were an invasion fleet now their space rubble. They are Grullers from another galaxy, just so you know we are about to land so we will talk at you later," Jake signaled Archie to cut them off.

"You know with NASA technology they can track us by reading the atmosphere and the wave we create like a boat in the water creates a wake," Archie informed Jake.

"So… why don't we do some laps until it's unreadable."

"That might work Jake. Okay let's give it a try," Archie went to a high speed and did a couple laps around the planet. He weaved left and right soon not even NASA could track 'em.

Written By
J.R. Wilson

52

Soon they set down about five hundred miles away, then they took off at low altitude and just cruised home at the speed of a normal small airplane. Archie announced proudly, "They can't track us now."

    "It's good to be back. Space is cool but it seems lonely, I could never be an astronaut," Jake declared.

Written By
J.R. Wilson

Chapter 9
Picnic Campout

Next day after breakfast everyone started showing up.
Trucks arrived loaded with picnic tables, another with eight
porta-potties. A flatbed trailer from a semi, they put by the barn
for the band. Big grills were pulled out of storage plus Jake's
two grills. Jake announced he was exhausted from the last
couple days so he's saddling up his horse and is going to ride
between the lake and the house so he can supervise and handle
any issues there are always issues.

"Tomorrow it's going to be crazy," Casey observed.
Casey and Rusty unloaded about twenty big tables and spread
out thirty picnic tables. People will bring side dishes, it's potluck
plus. They will cook hot dogs, burgers, polish sausage, and tri
tips.

"It's a lot of work but worth it," June pointed out, "Oh
Rusty can you put the trash cans around, so people don't have to
look for them?"

"Sure thing, come on Tech. You get to help," said Rusty.

"I can't. I'm working on getting electric to the flat bed for
the band tomorrow."

"I'll help ya Rusty," Jamie volunteered.

The Adventures of
Jake & Archie

That evening after dinner they sat on the porch and enjoyed a Colorado evening. Jake got a call it was the sheriff.

"Hey Jake, ready for tomorrow," the sheriff asked.

"We got a pig cooking. It will cook all night," Jake bragged, "The band is doing sound checks as we speak."

"The reason I'm calling is a prisoner was being extradited and during the international transfer to Canada. He escaped while on route. He's a mean one. There were three of them all male. They blew out the tires and shot and killed a guard and wounded two others. It all went down about fifty miles North of us. So… I thought with the picnic I should give you a heads up."

"We appreciate that. You're coming out for the picnic right," Jake asked a little worried.

"Yep, wouldn't miss it," said the sheriff.

"Ok talk to you in morning," Jake ended the call.

"Hey guys! Keep your eyes open tomorrow. The sheriff said a prisoner escaped during a transfer. He had help from three male individuals."

"Wow are they nearby," ask Jamie.

"I don't know… but it happened about fifty miles North us," Jake explained, "So it wouldn't be a bad idea to pack a weapon during the picnic. I know I will," Jake replied.

The next day people show up around eleven in the morning. Jake's sons were showing people where to pitch their tents. Some went to the lake and Casey was up there to show folks where they should set up camp, most were close to the lake and the dock. It's always that way. Some come to camp,

Written By
J.R. Wilson

some come just for the day for the food and dancing and of course the beer. Things were going along, pretty dang

good. Connie showed up later. When she finally arrived, Jamie showed her where to set up, he helped her with her tent, which happened to be right next to Jamie's.

"I'm so glad you showed up," Jamie said to Connie, "Are you hungry?"

Connie said, "I'm starving. It was an hour drive, and I haven't eaten anything today. As the Brits would say... I'm a bit peckish."

"Well, we have some food ready to eat and people brought sides, you stay here. I'll wait in line you rest from the drive," Jamie was being a gentleman.

"Ok, that sounds great, thank you kind sir," Connie was playing along.

Meanwhile Jake was telling June, "I believe we have more folks here this year."

"Every year it gets bigger," She agreed.

"Do you know where we are," the escaped prisoner asked.

"I'm not sure, I can't believe we lost the cops, there's a little town up ahead we can get gas," The driver reported.

They pulled into the gas station. The driver got out and started fueling up the car. Another car pulls up and the driver starts fueling.

"Why is this town so dead. Where is everyone," asked the driver of the getaway car.

"Everyone is out at the picnic camp out. Food, music, a lake for fishing, it's a great time. They do it a couple times a year, we are headed out there now," said the other driver.

Written By
J.R. Wilson

The Adventures of
Jake & Archie

"Do you mind if we follow you," asked the criminal.
"Not at all, no problem," replied the other driver.
They were off to the picnic.

The sheriff and his deputies were in plain clothes. Jake was talking to the sheriff, "Plain clothes, you guys look great. Go get some food there's plenty of everything. I think the wives out did themselves this year," Jake was happy to brag on their behalf. At the serving table there was a line. When Jake and the sheriff got their turn. June and Tony served them.

"June," Jake whispered, "Have you seen any folks you don't know maybe acting kind of weird?"

"No… not really. Why," June whispered back. They both seemed like they were acting a little weird. Tony could hear every word, shaking his head.

"Who are you looking for Pop," Tony whispered then laughed.

"Four criminals one is an escaped prisoner, but their probably miles away by now," Jake informed them trying to reassure them.

"Four guys? There was four men who I didn't know and when they were looking at the meat, I pointed out the sliced meat was tri tip and one of them asked what's tri tip. I told them it was prime beef. They each had some. I remembered thinking everyone in Colorado knows what tri tip is and then I let it go because we were so busy," Explained June.

"Do you remember what they looked like," Tony asked.

"Of course, their right over there," June pointed.

Tony suggested the three deputies go over to the four strangers' table and sit down with a plate, you know feel them out.

Written By
J.R. Wilson

57

"This is good, these folks know how to cook," The escaped criminal remarked.

"Yep, good chow. How long are we hanging around here," The driver asks, "We should keep moving."

"We will, there's a lot of sweet young things around here. What's the hurry."

"We aren't far enough away yet," The drive argued.

The convict saw Connie sitting by her tent, he walked over. The deputies were talking to the four men June pointed out. They got up and walked back to the serving table. The first deputy informed Tony and Jamie.

"I don't think that's them. In fact, I know it's not. They are guests of the table next to them they came in from Boulder," said the sheriff.

"What now Pop," Jamie asked.

"We watch and wait," Jake didn't want to panic anyone.

"Hello there, why is a fine-looking lady like yourself sitting alone?"

"I'm waiting for my date. He went to get us some food," replied Connie. She was a little nervous, this guy was creeping her out.

"He shouldn't have left a cutie like you alone. Maybe you should be with a real man," the convict continued. When Jamie came back with two plates of food the convict stood up and took both plates, "Thanks we were hungry go get some for yourself," Jamie was stunned. He looked at Connie; she stood up and got behind Jamie.

"This is your man?" said the convict, "Looks like a punk, granted a tall punk, but still a punk."

"I think you should leave… now," Jamie told the convict.

Written By
J.R. Wilson

"Really and what if we decide to stay," the convict stated in the threatening way.

Connie stepped out from behind Jamie, "Then you will get your ass kicked," Connie bragged.

"Ah, it's okay Connie let me handle this." Jamie said quietly.

"Yeah, you're going to get your man killed sweety," growled the convict. Tony came over. He saw Jamie was into something. Jamie and Tony wanted to take these guys out, but they had to get them away from the crowd. Someone could get hurt. Then the Convict and his three sidekicks flashed their guns to show that they meant business. Jamie noticed, the gun the convict was carrying was police issue pistol probably belonged to one of the guards they shot. That's when they were sure who these guys were. The convict grabbed Connie and pulled her to him then he pulled his gun and held it to her side.

"Now we're going to walk out of here and unless you want to bury your girlfriend you stay back," The convict was very serious. They headed to the front parking area. Jamie and Tony followed at a distance. Jamie looked over and saw his dad on the porch, and he could tell Pop knew what is going on. Jake had his Henry Golden Boy rifle. Both Tony and Jamie knew Pop never misses with his Henry, in hand.

When the four criminals reached their car Jamie and Tony stood up about fifty feet away from the criminals. Jamie could see Connie was looking back at them while she was being taken. Jamie kept stomping his left foot on the ground. Connie was confused why he was stumping his left foot, she wondered. Then Jamie hollered at the criminals. The convict turned and so did his partners and then, it hit Connie, what Jamie was doing. She stomped as hard as she could on the convict's foot. He gave out a yell and started to point his gun back at Connie but before

he could completely point it at her. In a split-second Jamie and
Tony Draw and shoot. Jamie hit the convict and Tony hit one of
the other three at the same time Jamie heard his Pop's Henry go
off and a third man fell. Jamie and Tony turned their attention
on the fourth they both shot, hitting him right in the head. Bullet
holes about one inch apart.

"Connie are you ok," Jamie ran up to her she was
shacking but unharmed.

"Wow," She said, "If this is how you do a picnic, I'm not
sure I want to go to dinner with you," She laughed sheepishly,
"By the way I'm still hungry."

Thay both laughed. The sheriff and his deputies came
running up, "Dog gone, you got 'em. When did you know it was
them?"

"Well… taking Connie was kind of a giveaway," Jamie
said. The boys gave a laugh.

Jake came running down from the house, "Y'all ok?
Nobody got hit," He looked at criminals laying there dead and
said, "At least nobody we care about got hit, right?"

"You know what Pop; we didn't need Archie for any of
this," said Tony. They laughed as if they weren't impacted by
what occurred.

"One thing I know for sure," Connie said, "This family
can shoot."

Hardly anyone noticed what happened, the music is loud,
people drinking and having a good ole time. The deputies
loaded up the body bags of the criminals. and hauled them off.
Casey, Rusty, and Tech. Walked over and looked at Jake.

Casey wanted to know "What the hell just happened"?

Jake smiled and said, "Come on, I'll get y'all a beer and
fill you in."

Written By
J.R. Wilson

The Adventures of
Jake & Archie

"Looks like we had an interaction with Canadian aliens after all," said Casey. Jake smiled and they indulged in few beers.

Written By
J.R. Wilson

The Adventures of
Jake & Archie

Chapter 10
Jamie Gets Some Help

One week later the boys went back to their units. They figured to save their leave for another emergency. They only used about nine days. It was good to get back to work. A few days later Jake gets a call.

"Hi Pop," said Jamie.

"Jamie what's up," Jake was happy to hear from Jamie.

"I have a little problem maybe you can help," asked Jamie.

"I would love to help what do you got," Jake was excited.

"I'm on a mission in South Africa. War lords are getting very aggressive, so my squad was sent to fix it. Thing is they're bringing in heavy stuff, tanks and artillery. We tried to hold them off. Right now, it's me and twelve other guys sitting between the war lords and the village. Maybe you and Archie could come over… soon… They're getting pretty damn aggressive around here," Jamie was nervous, Jake could tell his voice always gives him away.

Written By
J.R. Wilson

The Adventures of
Jake & Archie

"Send me your GPS. We're on our way," Jake jumped up and grabbed his sidearm and headed to the barn. Jake climbs into Archie and tells him what's going on. Within seconds Archie has the coordinates. They take off and head to Jamie. A few minutes and they are over Jamie's location. Still in stealth mode they head up towards the enemy.

"Man, this war lord has way too much heavy stuff. I count ten tanks, five troop carriers, a few supply trucks and six canons. Archie hit um with the EMP on the highest setting we are going to cook 'em first," Jake ordered.

Archie sets off the EMP. The whole convoy stops dead. The men are getting out checking things lifting hoods looking for their problem.

"Okay hover around so we hit them broad side," Jake instructs Archie. Once In position Archie cut loose. Only heavies and troop carriers, they left the supply trucks alone. They continued shooting troops because they weren't really troops, they were warlord mercenaries that rape and murder everywhere they go. Now stealing and murdering red cross workers.

Archie said, "There's nothing left alive down there."

Jake calls Jamie, "Ok son your good to go. Those slime balls are dead. Tell the villagers to get to those supply trucks. We didn't touch them."

"It should be safe," Archie said.

"No life down there. I'm going to check out the warlord's home base be right back," Jake hangs up and they head North. They see this mansion, so Archie scans the place and identifies five individuals. They are Warlords. They listen with Archies eavesdropping. They were talking about new territory and who gets what.

Written By
J.R. Wilson

The Adventures of
Jake & Archie

"To hell with this," Jake just opens up with both laser canons and soon that place was a pile of rubble.

Once back at the village Jake and Jamie were talking, "So how are you going to report all this Jamie? There are going to be questions you can't answer. Well... I should say you can answer them no one will believe you," Jake warned Jamie.

Jamie was sitting there trying to come up with an answer, "I don't know Pop."

Jake said, "Just tell them it's top secret no matter. What they say, stick with that," Jake thought for a minute, "I got an idea buy me some time, don't report right away. I'll call you in a bit," Jake and Archie took off, "Archie see if you can raise NASA."

"Jake, we have that guy you talked to. He's waiting already on the line," Archie said.

"Okay thanks Archie. Hello," Jake called out.

"Hello this is NASA. Who's this?"

"This is your friend from out passed the moon. I need to talk with the boss," said Jake.

"I am operations chief. I run the place," said the voice at NASA.

"Ok," Jake was satisfied, "Are you in a building at NASA."

"Yes," replied the voice or operations chief.

"Great walk outside and wave," said Jake.

"What? Walk outside and wave," questioned the voice.

"Yes," said Jake. Elevating his voice a bit. So Archie, still in stealth mode, climbed about two thousand feet so they could see everything.

Archie spotted a guy, "Look over there a guy waving."

"Great set down beside him," Jake opened the driver's door and got out. the guy standing there was somewhat

Written By
J.R. Wilson

surprised, seeing a man just appears out if nowhere, "Hi, I'm Jake. You are?"

"I'm in a state of shock. Jerry... I'm Jerry... yeah Jerry... operations chief."

"Ok, great get in, we are going for a ride. Don't worry we won't be long," said Jake.

Jake and Archie take Jerry for a ride. They flew around the planet and talked. Jerry was rambling question after question. Jake managed to settle him down. The inertia switch really got Jerry all worked up. So bottom line Jake worked out and agreement, Jake would communicate directly with Jerry and make himself and Archie available from time to time. But Jerry had to cover for Jamie and his top-secret excuse. Jerry made a couple calls to the White House. They made a three-way call with the Pentagon. A lot of questions came up which really didn't get any answers. But Jamie was off the hook for his report.

Jake dropped off Jerry then they headed back to Jamie in the village. Jake wanted to talk in person, he didn't want to broadcast their conversation. Jake and Archie arrive at the village. Jamie joined Jake in the car, and they had a conversation. Jake explained things and Jamie was impressed with what his Pop had pulled off. Aliens, War Lords, escaped criminals and NASA. It's been a busy couple of days.

"Time to go home," Jake declared.

Jake is one of those rare guys he puts family and his friends first. He can be hard to get along with, but you always want him with you in a tight spot. Archie is beginning to realize these qualities.

"Hey, Jake, I like you, you're a good man, but I think you're a little crazy we killed that war lord and his mercenaries like it was nothing, doesn't it bother you," Archie asked?

Written By
J.R. Wilson

The Adventures of
Jake & Archie

"I can't let it," Jake answered, "I know it's cold, but it must be this way. Those guys were deadly. Humans are more than one thing. Good, bad, deadly, loving, try to be fair, and a family man. Those are the main things which work for me. It is a requirement in this line of work you can't let the killing haunt you. Archie, you understand?"

"I think I'm beginning to... partner," said Archie.

Jake smiled, "Good. Now you know why I retired. Sometimes the lines got blurred. That's when I knew it was time to retire. June knew it too. I just wanted to come home and relax on the ranch and do ranch work maybe upgrade things."

"That's understandable Jake," Archie greed.

"You know weird and crazy has been finding me my whole life. I don't go looking for it, crazy always finds me," Jake speaking in an exaggerated high voice at the end pointing his finger up. Then he just started laughing. What the hell Aliens, Russians, war lords, escaped criminal, being retired I feel I've mellowed."

"Mellowed? You okay there Jake? You're not losing it are ya," asked Archie.

"I'm fine I just got to let go every now and then, no biggy," Jake sluffed it off, "Good we're home," as Archie set down in front of the house. Jake was ready to sleep for a week. June met him on the porch with a hug.

"Glad your home you must be hungry I got dinner on the stove."

"Sounds good hun," Jake was tired and hungry.

Written By
J.R. Wilson

66

Chapter 11
The Sheik Revisited

The next day Jake was sleeping in. June took a walk out to the barn. She approached Archie. Archie greeted her, "Good morning, June."

"Good morning, Archie," June went on, "Archie can we talk?"

"Of course, what's on your mind," Replied Archie.

"Well, I'm worried about Jake. His retirement has been challenging as of late. I was hoping you could try and make things... I don't know... easier on Jake somehow," June sounded concerned.

"Sure, anything I can do, I will," Archie went on to ask, "June can you tell me more about that sheik."

June stood there thinking, "Ok first, you have to know I wasn't exactly honest with you."

Archie questioned June, "What part were you not exactly honest with me?"

The Adventures of
Jake & Archie

"About a year ago the sheik came here to go skiing. Jake and his friends were at the resort and wanted to make sure the sheik was well taken care of. They even comped him for lift rides and some drinks. Anyway, Jake was visiting the sheik at the chalet. They were sitting around talking the sheik had about twenty young girls in their Arab attire sitting around him.

Jake asked, "Who are all these women?"

"These are some of my wives. I didn't bring them all," answered the sheik.

"Some of them look very young," observed Jake. Jake noticed three of the girls were eyeballing him when the sheik wasn't looking, he was more interested in his hookah he was puffing away on. Jake blurted out, "How many of you girls speak English? Just raise your hand if you do," Three girls raised their hands they were looking at the sheik fearfully. Jake said, "Don't look at him look at me," Jake asks the first girl, "Do you want to be a wife of the sheik?"

She replied, "No," The other two also said, "No," In no uncertain terms.

The sheik said, "You cannot do this, these are my possessions."

"Listen up Sheik you're in America, we don't own people in this country and I'm pretty sure England feels the same way. You're really starting to piss me off sheik," Jake said angrily, "I really want to put a couple bullets in you, human trafficking, kidnapping young girls."

"Wait…" said the sheik, "I didn't kidnap anyone."

"No but you create a market for kidnappers you piece of crap. Oh… to hell with this. Guys take this low life scum outside and end him," said Jake.

"Okay boss," said Casey.

Written By
J.R. Wilson

The Adventures of
Jake & Archie

"No… no. Wait you can't kill me, Jake. We are friends," pleaded the sheik.

"I don't need friends like you," Jake snapped back at the sheik, "If you want to leave here alive. Write down the other sheiks and the names of the traffickers."

"Okay… but will this make us friends again," begged the sheik.

"I must consider all that's happened. It doesn't look good for you."

One of the girls behind Jake whispered in Jake's ear, "There were two other girls that were American. They wouldn't conform to the sheik's demands. They fought and struggled. So, he cut their throats right in front of us to scare us."

"Ok that's it… load the girls in the hotel bus. Take 'em to the airport there will be a chinook waiting there to get them home," Jake ordered, "We will bring the Sheik."

The Sheik hollered at his guards to kill them! Casey and Rusty quickly drew the weapons. All you heard was a series of muffled pop's. Three guards laid on the floor dead, "You are worthless," yelled the sheik at his dead guards. On the bus Jake, Casey and Rusty hauled the sheik to the airport.

"Your religion says there are seventy virgins waiting for you. Are you excited to meet them," Jake laughed, "You know that seventy virgin's thing… I've given it a lot of thought. I think your God is playing a trick on y'all. See seventy virgins… they probably have been coddled, spoiled and pampered. You show up and one of two things will happen. First, they tell you, 'We are virgins, that's who we are. That's our identity and we aren't giving it up for the likes of you.' Then you must listen to seventy girls' prattle on wanting this and that. Second. flip side of the coin, they give in. For the next seventy days you deal with one a day, she is going to cry from pain and bleed. I don't think

Written By
J.R. Wilson

it's going to be enjoyable for anyone. New set of sheets every day," Jake was laughing, "But you get to go through that sixty-nine more times. Not a fun date… and the second time they will lay there wondering why you're doing this to her as she stares at the ceiling sobbing. Now You must deal with women and their cycles. Seventy women fifty-two weeks a year. You're going to be going through hell all year. Can they get pregnant? If so, if just half get pregnant that's thirty-five screaming kids. Yeah… doesn't sound like heaven to me sounds more like hell. It would make more sense to me if you had seventy hookers waiting for you. At least they have experience. But hey, that's your God not mine, thank goodness," they arrive at the airport.

"Oh, look a second chinook what now," pointed out Casey.

Jake walks over to the second helicopter, "Why two," Jake ask the pilot.

"Last time we came you needed two. One for body bags and one for prisoners," the pilot remarked.

"Okay… an unfortunate mistake. We need you to take us up with that piece of crap sheik," Then Jake went on, explaining what the sheik had done and how he killed two young American girls. Making an example out of them and doing it in front of the rest of the girls so they live with that on their minds for the rest of their lives.

The pilot said, "Let's go," with considerable enthusiasm.

"Alright load up," yelled Jake.

When the helicopter was at about eight thousand feet Casey opened the side door and the sheik started crying and begging.

"Please Jake! We are friends… we are friends don't do this," cried the sheik.

Written By
J.R. Wilson

The Adventures of
Jake & Archie

"Did those girls cry and beg and you killed them for no good reason," Jake growls. Just like that he pushed the Sheik out of the helicopter. Jake Yelled at the Sheik as he went out the door, "GOOD LUCK WITH THOSE SEVENTY VIRGINS," Casey laughed, he thought that was pretty good and justified.

Rusty asked, "Do you think God will hold this one against us?"

"Our God won't care. Look at the religious wars they had back in day. Besides he worshipped a God who tells them when you die, you will have sex and promises virgins. Yeah, we're ok," Jake reassured them.

"So that's the story, Archie what do think," June asked.

"Well… sounds like your crooks," Archie pointed out.

June laughed, "Yeah, I can understand you're thinking that. But we are only crooks to the crooked," June laughed.

"Say there's an injustice, if Jake and the boys run across it, they deal with it. Jake, when there's trouble, he will always move forward never back. He's been that way since he was a kid," said June, "So here's the clincher the deposits kept going in for about three more months then they stopped. Jake and the boys went back over seas and robbed the sheik one last time but this time they didn't give it back," June proclaimed.

"What happened to the loot," Archie asked trying to sound cool.

"Well, it's in two large safety deposit boxes at the bank. Gold coins, gold bars, antiques all in gold. a couple hundred million safely tucked away. An emergency fund for the city," June proudly stated.

"What happened to the list the sheik gave Jake," Archie was curious.

Written By
J.R. Wilson

71

The Adventures of
Jake & Archie

"Oh… yeah… Jake got it to interpole, Homeland
Security, FBI, and the CIA he figured, give it to them all and let
them compete over who gets there first. If they slip by, the NSA
has a list as well," June explained, "See we are the good guys.
They caught the traffickers, the sheiks are using government
protection it's costing them a whole lot," June was laughing,
"I've got to get back inside, Jake will be waking up soon. Need
to get him some breakfast, see ya later Archie."
    And with that, June headed back into the house.

Written By
J.R. Wilson

Chapter 12
The Adventure Continues

It's been a few days since June had her talk with Archie.
Jake is in the barn with Archie checking out the trunk, "Wow
this trunk is weird. You open this door and walk down steps and
I'm in a strange house. How is that possible?"

"It's a different realm. That house is your place for
storage or rest, it has a sitting room, kitchen, and bathroom. The
sitting room has a screen like a theater; accept you're seeing
what the driver sees. Nothing can get you there unless they
crawl into my trunk. The door in the trunk is a portal," Archie
finished.

"Very cool," said Jake excited, "I'll be back," as he ran
to the house. A few minutes go by, and Jake comes out with a
wheelbarrow full of guns, ammo and explosives just an array of
goodies.

"Might as well be prepared. Plus, I won't have all those
explosives in the house or barn," Jake was having fun, "It's like
have a traveling ammo dump that can't hurt us," Jake went on
loading the weapons into the trunk. Jake thought he should go
outside. He wanted to see what's out there. He continued his
walk and walked right into a force field. When he hit it, it

Written By
J.R. Wilson

knocks him back on his butt. Jake got up and went back in the house.

"So that's why the stuff is safe. A force field, great stuff," Jake smiled, "I like it."

Archie laughed, "You didn't give me a chance to tell you about the force field."

Jake made another trip to the house and brought more stuff out. You would think he's moving out. June was watching and was wondering what the hell Jake was doing.

"You want me to pack you a suitcase or were you just going to leave," June remarked half laughing under her breath.

"Let me show you this. Come out to the barn," Jake said like a schoolboy.

"Ok, honey just give me a minute," June said while washing up. June walked toward the barn when Casey and the guys joined her.

"What's up June," Casey inquired.

"Jake is all excited about something. I haven't seen him like this in years," June replied.

They got to the barn Jake was nowhere to be seen.

"Jake," June yelled, "Jake where are you?"

"Right here," Jake answered. The four of them turned and saw Jake raising up out of Archies trunk.

"What the heck. How are you doing that," June was in shock.

Jake laughed and said, "Come over here and take a look."

They all went around to the trunk and saw the door that leads down some stairs.

"What is that?" June asked.

"It's a portal to another realm. We can use this portal to haul everything we need wherever we go. It's a fully functional, house bedrooms, kitchen, bathroom, and a viewing room where it has a screen like a theater. Except you're watching what we see out the front windshield."

"Where is this," Casey asked, while going down the stairs.

"As far as I can tell it's someplace that is impossible to get to and is protected by a force field. the only way to get there is through the door in the trunk," Jake was filling them in, "Our own private getaway," Jake laughed, "It's another planet in a foreign realm. I can't wait to see what's next anyway. I stored most of our gear, weapons and ammo. I figured its safer there and safer for us."

Everyone went down the stairs, checking the house. Rusty did the same thing. Jake did, walking into the force field. Rusty ended up like Jake on his butt.

June was looking around the house, "How did they know to build a house like this?" She wondered out loud.

Jake said, "When they gave us the car, they scanned our planet to see how we live and duplicated what they thought would be comfortable for us humans."

While the group was sitting around the kitchen table drinking a few beers, they didn't notice the portal was gone, it had been closed. Archie pulls out of the barn and takes off for deep space. He is trying to get deep enough to open a larger portal. Whenever anyone opens a portal, it must be in deep space because they are leaving one galaxy and going to another. The time difference between the galaxies creates a paradox that affects out to five hundred thousand miles. That's why deep space, the paradox created doesn't affect life on other planets, the waves start to dissipate almost immediately it takes the full five hundred thousand miles before it's gone.

The Adventures of
Jake & Archie

Jake realizes the door is shut. He starts pounding on the door, "Archie, open the door!" Jake hollers again, "Archie! Archie!" Jake turns and looks at the group and says, "Something is wrong. Archie and I have talked when I'm in here, he is always in full contacted with me."

June asked, "What do we do Jake?"

"I don't know," Jake replied, "Archie, damn you! Talk to me!"

Archie replied, "Keep quiet!"

"Archie what the hell is going on," Jake wanted answers.

"I said be quiet," Archie snapped back. That was the last time Archie spoke. Jake kept trying but nothing. Archie was silent.

"Maybe we can blow the door," Casey inquired.

"No, if there's one thing I know, we don't know what's out there. We could be anywhere, even outer space. It would be nice, when door opens there's air, wherever we are," Jake informed them.

"Man, it started off being a nice day," Rusty pondered, "How long do we wait?"

"Don't know, we have enough food for a few days. Might as well relax nothing we can do," Jake seems like it was all going to work out.

Archie was starting to phase and the car slipped through a portal.

Written By
J.R. Wilson

Chapter 13
Where The Hell Are We?

Back at the ranch Connie pulled up. Bullet their chocolate lab came running up happy to see Connie, "Hi boy, you being a good dog?" Connie pet Bullet as she walked up to the porch. Connie knocked at the door but there was no answer. She walked around on the porch of the house with Bullet at her side, "Huh," she said, "They were expecting me," she said to Bullet. Connie checks the crew houses and both barns but nothing. She headed back to the house and tried the doorknob. It was unlocked so she went in. Calling out for June and Jake and then she searched the bedrooms. In the kitchen she saw the coffee was still on. Bullet was standing by his food bowl, and it was empty, so Connie fed him.

"Here you go boy you must be hungry," Bullet was wagging his tail. *This is strange doors unlocked coffee still hot. Where are they?* Connie was thinking. She decided to call the sheriff. She knew that he was a close friend to Jake. A voice came over the phone.

"Hello sheriff's office."

"Yes, this is Connie is the sheriff in?" Connie asked.

Written By
J.R. Wilson

"Speaking, how can I help you, Connie?" said the sheriff.

She filled him in on the situation. He decided it was odd, so he told her to "stay put" he was on his way.

While Jake was concerned, he knew one thing for sure, "Okay everyone vest up with plates and June that includes you. When that door opens, we need to be ready for anything," Jake was in commando mode and wasn't taking any chances as long as his wife was with them. Jake went back to the door, it seemed like hours. They had been in this house.

Pretty soon they heard Archie say, "Where the... How did..."

"Archie, where are we?" Jake yelled, "get us out of here!"

"Jake? Is that you where are you?" Archie was a little out of it.

"We're in the trunk open the door," Jake demanded.

"Not a problem," Archie said still confused. The door opened and Jake went up the stairs cautiously, rifle in hand he stepped out to see a different world.

"What the heck... where are we? Come up guys its breathable air," said Jake.

"Are you sure its good air," June called out.

"Yeah, pretty sure. I'm not dead so that's a good indicator. Archie you, okay? Why are we here? And why wouldn't you talk to me?" Jake inquired.

"Well, I don't recall anything. Last thing I remember we were in the barn, and you were loading stuff into the realm house. Wait, I think I figured out where we are," said Archie.

Written By
J.R. Wilson

The Adventures of
Jake & Archie

"Yeah… so did I," replied Jake. He saw a familiar figure walking towards them, "Hey commander what are we doing here," Jake ask very annoyed.

"Hello, welcome to our planet. I saw your car approaching, we hailed you but there was no answer. You weren't in stealthy mode and there was no one in the car. That's when I knew something wasn't right. We picked up a signal as you were drawing near. It comes from here and was directed at your car. We believe it was controlling Archie. Apparently, it's been transmitted to Archie since day one when we gave you the car. We weren't aware of this because we weren't looking for it. The signal was on a band we don't use or look at very often. But when you were approaching it became clear," said the commander.

"Okay… so what now," Jake asked still very upset.

The commander walked around to the front of Archie, "Archie pop your hood," the commander saw something that shouldn't be there. He reached in and removed a small box, "This is it. That's why Archie and the Nanites couldn't detect it or stop it. The box wasn't part of Archie's system, yet it could access and control Archie. Now it's no longer a problem," the commander reassured Jake.

"Well… I have a problem. Who did this? How and why," Jake insisted.

"It's a long story so I'll give you the short version," they were walking to a building where they entered a room and sat down around a table. This planet is very colorful, bright colored buildings and small aircraft flying around at low altitude, "About seventy percent of this planet is made up of scientists the rest is your artist and builders and farmers etcetera. About three years ago one of our deep space surveyors came across some foreign substance. They brought it back and we put it in

Written By
J.R. Wilson

the hands of six of our smartest scientists. They worked in a closed environment, just them in a sealed room. When they opened the container, some steam started coming out of it. Alarms went off and safety protocol was initiated. The air was sucked out and it seemed like we got it in time the scientists were fine. But in the weeks to come everything started to change. The six scientists were acting oddly. Not showing up for work. When they did show they were ignoring other scientists they were becoming very hostile. Not doing their job just being a nuisance getting into fights. This was a problem because none of this is in our nature. We had to do something with them. We took them to a facility that would treat them and keep them in confinement," the commander finished.

"I thought you said the short story," Jake pointed out.

"Yes sorry," said the commander, "Anyway they broke out about three weeks ago."

"How did they do that? You're supposed to be a very advanced civilization," Jake was being kind of snide.

"Yes, your right that was my first question when they broke out," the commander agreed.

The men running the facility answered, "When you lock up six of our top scientists it was a simple thing for them to overcome door locks."

"Okay, so where are you on catching them," ask Casey.

"We have had no sign of them. We are working on tracing the signal to its source, since we just found out about the signal. It could take some time," replied the commander.

"How long do you think," Jake asked.

"Oh… a couple minutes to a couple hours remember these guys are geniuses," the commander reconfirmed. Archie asked Jake to go to the trunk.

Written By
J.R. Wilson

The Adventures of
Jake & Archie

"What's in the trunk Archie," Jake asked. Jake was unaware Archie had a little surprise for him.

"Look in the front left side of my trunk and open the door on the box," said Archie.

"What is this," Jake was holding a small device, "Looks like a taser it's so small. Molded grip nice, so is it a taser?"

Archie replied, "Your right it's kind of like a taser except it's very powerfully you zap a human, and it will throw them ten feet or more, if you hold it on them for a few seconds game over. Just thought if you get into hand-to-hand combat it might come in handy."

"Commander, you say they broke out three weeks ago, what day," Jake's gut was getting that old feeling, "Was it before we got the car?"

"Oh yeah, it was the day before," commander answered, looking like he just thought of something.

Jake inquired, "Archie, you said you don't remember a thing, is there a record or history in your memory that's void or blank?"

"Yes, about three hours are totally blank," Archie seemed nervous.

"Does your GPS keep a record of where you've been," Jake was doing his investigating thing.

"Yes, but we know what happened I brought you guys here," Archie replied a little confused.

"Do you have any other blanks in your memory? Say three weeks ago," Jake was digging deeper.

"Now that you mention it there's four hours unaccounted for a day before I was delivered to you."

"Archie let me see the GPS from that day," Jake ordered.

The commander joined in, "You said earlier that there's a force field around the house Jake. Isn't that what you said?"

Written By
J.R. Wilson

The Adventures of
Jake & Archie

"Yeah, I guess it was for security. Right," Jake was looking at the GPS on Archie's dash.

"We didn't install a force field," the commander went on, "There's no reason, that planet is safe."

"So,who installed it," Archie asked, he was wondering because he didn't know, and he should know.

"Look at this. This shows you in the lab then you leave and go halfway around your planet and set down for about two hours then back to the lab," Jake was confounded, "Archie you aided them in their escape. You didn't know what you were doing, and that's when they installed that little box," Jake continues, "I'll bet these scientists installed the force field at that time. So… are we supposed to think the force field was there not to keep folks outside the house. But to keep folks in, so the scientists could hide anywhere in the realm," Jake was thinking out loud.

"That means they're still in there or they are at that place on the other side of the planet," the commander pointed out.

"Can you remove the force field," Jake hoped, "If you can we will do a search in the realm maybe we get lucky. Let's get back in there I need to look around when something doesn't smell right. These guys are smart. I'm not so sure we are going to find anything," Jake pointed out.

Back in the realm Jake and the commander were working on the force field.

"It is generated from the center of the roof. We need to get in the attic," the commander said. Jake was thinking the commander seemed very familiar with this force field.

"Let's get up there," Jake was inpatient.

Once they got to the attic the commander pulled out a device and cut off the force field. Jake said a bit confuse, "That was easy, I figured it would take a while or we would blow that

Written By
J.R. Wilson

blasted thing up, but you knew just what to do commander,
that's lucky."

"I've had some experience dealing with force fields," the
commander bragged.

"Alright my team and I will check this place over... but
good." Jake continues.

"I can help," the commander offered.

"No! My team and I work together. We know each other
well enough. We do things without saying a word, a new guy
would upset our routine. Someone could get hurt, if we have to
think about you or anyone new to our procedure," Jake snapped.
He wasn't sure he could trust the commander. This whole
situation had the hair on the back of Jakes neck standing up.
That's a signal Jake doesn't ignore, "Alright men, when we get
outside head left to the tree line. We will patrol from the trees
stay out of the pasture," Jake instructed.

Once they got to the trees Jake sat the guys down and
said, "Look I didn't want the commander to know what we're
doing. Something doesn't add up. I'm going to find out what's up
with all this. Casey you and Tech stay back here, Rusty and I
will check the trees. I'm thinking maybe they want us to go deep
in the realm, and they lay back and duck into the house. So,
heads on a swivel, keep your eyes up and stay alert. Let's go!"

Written By
J.R. Wilson

Chapter 14
The Search

Jake and Rusty have gone about a hundred yards into the trees when they spot a clearing and what appears to be some sort of shelter, six of them. Then they saw something they weren't expecting. Youngsters playing and laughing then they see a female.

"Must be their mom," Rusty whispered to Jake, "What is this boss," Rusty asked.

"I'm not sure but let's find out. Stand ready I'll go in you cover me," Jake commanded.

"Copy that," Rusty obeyed.

Jake stands up and walks in slowly, rifling locked and loaded. He was going easy because he wasn't sure how he would be received. The kids spot him and just stand and look. They had never seen a human, but even with his rifle the kids didn't seem afraid of him.

"Howdy," Jake was trying to be friendly. The kids didn't move there were five of them, maybe they feel safe because of their numbers. Out came three of the scientists walking toward Jake.

Written By
J.R. Wilson

"Hello. Who are you and why are you here," one of them said.

"Well, we are looking for you," Jake answered.

"We? I only see you," Jake waved his hand and out came Rusty.

"We don't want to harm you we just want to talk," Jake turned to Rusty, "Go get Casey and Tech bring 'em here."

"You got it boss," Rusty said, as he headed back the way they came. When the rest of the guys arrived. They had an interesting story to tell.

"Boss the commander and six of his men showed up. They didn't see us. They headed off to the right side of the pasture. I don't understand why they came in here," Casey went on to say, "It's like they wanted to sneak up on us."

"I'm pretty sure that's exactly what they are up to. That's the reason I wanted you guys to wait there. I want you three to take positions to cover us. I will deal with the commander. Casey gets the grenade launcher ready it might be over kill, but just in case. Better to have it and not need it. I don't care what happens to the commander's men, but I want him alive or close to it," Instructed Jake, "All you scientists and your families are going to need to hide. Do you have a place that's secure," Jake asked.

"Yes, we have a backup place that's hidden," The scientist assured Jake.

"Ok, good we are going to set up to take these guys. I will wait in the shelter and give them a surprise," Jake was getting into his combat mode. It has been a while, but it was coming back to him in waves.

After about an hour Jake heard a familiar voice, "Jake... Jake! You here? Jake come out we can talk," the commander hollered.

Written By
J.R. Wilson

The Adventures of
Jake & Archie

Jake got on his two-way radio, "Guys you got 'em?"

"We are totally set. We have five of them dialed in one is missing and the commander is in the camp area," Casey informed Jake.

"Take 'em out. The last one will show when the action starts," said Jake.

"Copy that boss," Casey acknowledged. The guys are retired but they muster up, quick and decisive action. Some hand to hand, some quiet pops from silencers. It was a few seconds they were done.

"Now what," said Rusty, "I'm Jacked up! This got over to quick," then the sixth guy fired at them, they turned and fired back, they all three hit him.

"I hear ya brother me to," Casey was wound up as well, "Let's see what Jake does with the commander it should be good."

The three of them went down to the camp. The commander was delivered by two of the scientists who witnessed the conflict. They we're excited about having the commander under their control. When everyone was gathered at the camp social area. Jake stared at the commander.

Then he started in on him, "You lied to me…I trusted you! And you have just been full of crap! These folks told me… two hundred years! You have been running things here for two hundred years! That's insane! These six scientists told me they built the car over eight months of earth time. Not forty-eight hours. You wanted to unload this prototype because it scares you? Amazing you're such a coward, you were taking credit for the car, like you were doing this because of my truck. All lies," Jake was on a roll.

"But… they… could build hundreds I couldn't have that! We would lose control; I would lose control!" The commander

Written By
J.R. Wilson

looked confused and said, "I must keep the serenity. People here love me!"

"You betrayed the trust to your people and to me. I TRUSTED YOU! I only trust seven people, and you were making the list. But you betrayed a huge trust," Jake was getting fired up, "Where I'm from trust is a big deal. We don't break a trust... well we try not to. There are different levels of trust! Ya know! You trust your dog not to pee on the floor, but he does so you put him outside and clean it up! You trust your kids not to screw up, but they do, and you help clean it up. You trust your wife you took vows with not to screw around, well that one can make you crazy. My point is you really messed up! A whole planet! Now I must do something about it! Men escort these folks to the house."

"Okay boss," Casey replied. As the group headed into the trees, Jake waited till they were out of sight.

"Archie, are you taking video and audio?" Jake was curious.

"Well... yes, I always do," Archie replied.

"Well kill the uplink video and audio for two minutes, okay?"

"Ok bye," Archie said sort of sad.

"Bye," said Jake. He waited a second or two then he fired his judge three times. The commander went down like a lump then Jake put one more in the commander's head. Then Jake grabbed his gear and fast walked to catch up with the group. Archie came back on.

"Jake you there," asked Archie.

"Yea I'm here," replied Jake.

"Is everything ok? Where's the commander," Archie sounded a little worried.

Written By
J.R. Wilson

The Adventures of
Jake & Archie

Jake just kept walking and said, "He didn't make it. Archie do you always take video?"

Archie replied, "Yes," nervously.

"Do you record all of it," Jake continues, "You don't send it out online did you?"

"Ahh... umm... yes, I record it but its only for our eyes," Archie was very nervous you hear it in his voice.

"You don't send it out, did you... no you wouldn't do that that... would you," said Jake.

Archie reluctantly answered "Well... uh... I did put it online but only for this planet. I thought it would be alright. They needed to see what the commander had been doing."

"Great," Jake said under his breath, "Wonder how this is going to play out," Jake catches the group and the first thing one of the youngsters ask.

"Where's that commander guy?"

Jake looked around the group; they were looking at him as they continued to walk. Without changing his expression Jake looked at them and said, "He died it was sudden," Then he smiled a little, the group started to laugh. Remembering that's what Jamie said to him, it's honest and direct. See you can learn things from your kids.

Another kid said, "What were the shots we heard there was three and then one."

"Ah... I was checking my gun to make sure it worked, and it would scare anything away that might be around," Jake was smug he thought that was a good answer.

"But there's nothing in this realm," One of the kids pointed out.

Jake looked around, "Good point. Wow... you make it real hard to lie about," Jake said laughing. They all laughed.

"Hey Jake," One the scientists wanted to talk to him.

Written By
J.R. Wilson

Jake responded, "Yeah what's up?"

"You know the people that were disappearing, well, I know where they are."

"You do? How? Okay…Where are they?" Jake challenged.

"They are all at the confinement center where we were. Anyone who ran against the commander or made him mad or disagreed with him. You have two hundred years of folks that did something that didn't sit right with the commander. There are over a thousand prisoners who did nothing but piss off that ass."

"We'll set them free," Jake demanded, "I will see to it, if necessary," Jake talking to the scientists.

"Why did you put a tracer in the car? It took over Archie and he didn't know what was happening while navigating deep space that seems dangerous," said Jake.

"We didn't put anything like that on the car it must have been the commander or one of his lackeys," replied the scientist.

Jake was surprised, "So that box he removed from Archie was nothing? Hey Archie, you still there," Jake asked.

"Of course, sir," Replied Archie.

"If you are transmitting then everyone saw the conflict that means the scientists could have been watching and knew we were outside their shelter. Yet they did nothing to prepare a defense. They let their kids play outside. Very curious," Jake was trying to understand.

"Or they didn't have their monitor on and just didn't know," Archie reasoned.

"Archie, I think you need to run a self-diagnostic. Make sure there's nothing controlling you," Jake requested.

"Ok Jake copy that," said Archie.

Written By
J.R. Wilson

The Adventures of
Jake & Archie

When they arrived at the house Jake sent June through first. Then his men, then he went through before the scientists he wanted to make sure they weren't harassed by anyone. As Jake passed through the portal, he could hear what sounded like a crowd. When he appeared, the noise went off the charts. The Amorlites were celebrating the end of the commander, and they went wild when they saw Jake. He was their hero. After two hundred years of dictatorship, they were free. When the six scientists appeared, the crowd got louder these guys were loved and the commander knew it. When he locked them up. No news or any reports of them being locked up. It was like they disappeared, which the commander was playing up, as if they did something terrible and they went into hiding. Which was a lie. But all's well that ends well.

An Amorlite walked up to Jake and handed him what appeared to be a remote control, "This is what the commander used to control the car. He had it added right before they shipped you the car."

"Who are you," Jake asked.

"I was second in command. Now with the commander gone it's on me to keep things running."

"If I were you, I would be looking for a new job. The folks who disappeared are fine and in the confinement prison. They are being released. So, there's probably a vote in your planets future. This is no time for you to make folks upset with your leadership," said Jake. The Amorlite nodded in agreement.

Jake and June along with Casey, Tech and Rusty loaded up in Archie and headed for home, "Archie I have the remote the commander was using on you."

"Thank you, Jake, you are going to destroy it, right," Archie asked.

Written By
J.R. Wilson

The Adventures of
Jake & Archie

"Sure, as soon as I get a chance," said Jake. The phasing was very interesting as they changed galaxies.

"Wow, that was weird," said June.

Casey didn't like the feeling it gave him, "I can live without doing that again."

The guy's kind of chuckled at his remarks. After a couple hours Archie was on approach, "Hey guys... looks like the sheriff's and Connie's car are out front of the house," Archie announced.

Written By
J.R. Wilson

Chapter 15
It's Good to be Home

Archie was making his approach. Jake announced, "I believe we are going to have to include the sheriff and Connie into our little circle of knowledge about Archie. Is everyone okay with that?"

They all agreed it was time and important.

"Ok Archie, come in from the front and remove the stealth so they can see us land. I'm calling the sheriff," said Jake. He dialed his phone, "Hello sheriff, how you are doing?"

"Where are you? We've been worried sick about you. Is June with you guys," the sheriff asked in a panic.

"Everybody's fine I need you and Connie to go out to the front porch and keep watching," Jake instructed.

"Okay, what are we looking for," the sheriff was curious. As the sheriff was asking, he got his answer Archie removed the stealth and Connie, and the sheriff got an eye full. Archie landed and pulled up in front.

"God it's good to be home," June said relieved.

They all talked, the sheriff and Connie were brought up to speed. Connie filled in Jake on how she and the sheriff fed the critters. The happiest one of everybody was Bullet. He was dancing around and barking. He is a happy dog.

The next day everyone was doing chores. Things seem back to normal. June was making lunch for Jake and the guys. They sat at the table eating and looking at each other.

Casey broke the silence, "I still can't believe what happened to us. It was cool and at the same time freaky… Did that really happen."

Jake laughed, "You don't know how many times I've asked that same question. Yes, it really happened."

Later that day it was just starting to get dark. Jake was sitting in the barn talking with Archie. While Jake and Archie were talking an SUV pulled in the driveway three fellas got out and walked towards the Barn.

"Can I help you," Jake asked.

"Yes, we are FBI," one of the men said in a heavy Ukrainian Accent.

Jake was getting intel from Archie. Archie had scanned and x-rayed the strangers, "Jake that guy has a Homeland Security badge and interpole badge and CIA and NSA. I believe they're fakes."

Jake laughed, "So you're FBI, are ya?"

"Yes, we are here to impound your car," the so-called FBI agent answered.

"Why do you want my car," Jake was musing.

"We have had reports that your car was involved in a crime."

Jake was still laughing, "You know if you would have pulled out that interpole badge I might have been fooled longer than a minute. Your accent is not FBI," Jake is still laughing.

"Never mind that, we are taking the car," the FBI goon said in a direct and stern voice.

Written By
J.R. Wilson

The Adventures of
Jake & Archie

"You guys found it easy to pull up in my driveway, walk over to my barn and make threats," Jake informed them, "But how do you plan to leave?"

Now, when they walked up, they saw Casey, Tech, and Rusty sitting at the other end of the barn, on a couch watching TV. Now they looked again the guys had disappeared. The first FBI agent pulled his coat back so Jake could see his gun. Then the other two did the same.

"Oh my, you have guns, oh no," Jake was playing, "Archie they have guns."

"Who you talking to," The agent asked.

Then Archie fired up his motor and with the help of the nanites he revved his motor, and a huge blast of air came off the back of Archie. The three fake agents went flying back on to the pavement.

Jake was having fun, "Look Archie that one flew thirty maybe thirty-two feet. The other two are around twenty feet. But that thirty-two is a record!"

Jake was still having fun. Casey, Tech, and Rusty were now standing over the three with shot guns pointed at them on the ground. Jake wanted to know why they really wanted the car, but they weren't talking.

So, Casey had a great idea, "Make them strip Jake."

"Good plan… okay boys, strip! Leave the underwear on. No one wants to see that!"

When they finished getting underdressed, "Okay boys you can leave now," Jake said they headed for their SUV, "Oh no you're walking back the truck stays here."

"But… it's a rental," the leader stated defeated.

"Start walking," Casey ordered.

Written By
J.R. Wilson

94

Tech got on the phone to their guy in D. C. He asks for a helicopter pick up. Three men on the county road walking to town. Easy to spot because they're in their underwear.

"I wonder who sent them," Jake was thinking, "Maybe they had ties to the Russians that attacked us. Well, the guys in D. C. will find out."

Chapter 16
Russians Again… but it's not?

"Russians… I don't know, these guys were very direct. Coming right to the house and try to pass themselves off as a Feds," Jake felt like something was different about this, "I think we might have new players. I believe the Russians passed off information to another family hoping they can do what the Russians couldn't."

Casey agreed, "I think this is another mafia type… but not Russian. Just feels like that."

"Ok, lets figure something new for defense, if they know where I am, then they might know about our buried surprises. Something they won't expect," Jake's mind was going a mile a minute, "I think… I have a plan," So Jake began to lay it out for everyone, which include the help from the sheriff's department. In the days to follow they prepared, with motion sensors and night vision cameras added to the county road leading to the ranch driveway. They were covered for any intruders.

Jake started reminiscing, "Remember when Bullet was our early warning system, that dog would bark at folks he didn't know if he knew them, he would just sit on the porch and stare to make sure he was right," Jake was laughing. Bullet was standing by Jake tail wagging, he knew they were talking about him he probably thought they were going hunting, "Best chocolate lab ever. Hell, best dog ever," Jake declared. Bullet agreed. Jakes cell was going off, it's the sheriff.

"Jake, three black SUVs full of guys coming your way. We will follow at a distance."

Written By
J.R. Wilson

The Adventures of
Jake & Archie

"Copy that, see you soon," all the guys got into position, Jake climbed into Archie. They drove out to the county road and parked in the middle. Blocking the road. Jake gets out and stands next to the driver's side front tire. He's watching them approach on his tablet. The night vision cameras are working great.

Archie says, "I got you covered Jake."

"Okay… thanks bud," Jake answered. He knew Archie had him covered, "Okay guys, eyes up here. Here they come," Jake announced. He stood his ground, when the SUVs appeared. Jake put his hand up trying to get them to stop, which they did.

"All of you look to my left," Jake held his hand out pointing at Casey and they saw him behind a .50 caliber chain gun. Then Jake said, "look to my right," and there was a deputy behind another .50 caliber chain gun, "Now we got snipers watching, so don't be stupid. Get out hands up, leave your weapons in the vehicles. Walk forward and keep the hands high."

They lined up and the guys ran down and started cuffing them a chinook landed in the pasture a few minutes later and they marched those Ukrainians to the helicopter.

One of them said, "How did you know?"

Jake answered, "This is my home, and nothing happens here without me knowing."

Tech walked up, "We got three in the trees, they weren't so lucky you might send a couple guys with body bags over there," Tech went on, "Oh… you have to call back D.C. they have some information for your boss."

Jake pulled out his cell and called D. C. Jake let it ring a few times and a familiar voice answered.

"Hey Jake, we don't talk enough, seems like Tech is the only one I talk with."

Written By
J.R. Wilson

"Yeah… well… I'll correct that," Jake replied.

The voice said, "Nice," Jake was thinking, he would have Casey start calling instead of Tech. He kind of laughed to himself.

"What's this info you got for me?" asked Jake.

"Those first three you sent us, we identified. They are Ukrainian but not from the government. These guys have their own family, and they received info from that Russian family you took out."

"I kind of figured that out myself, you got anything I don't already know," Jake asked.

"Yes," respond the voice, "They aren't going to quit. They will keep coming, now that they know where you live."

"I need all the info you can get on this family especially where they live and where they're based." Jake requested.

"You got it, I will send it to your email," the voice hung up. *Kind of rude… and he wonders why I don't call him,* Jake thought.

Meanwhile, as all the stuff was going down on the county road. Tech was sitting in the living room with a baseball game on. He's using a tablet. It was set up with night vision to see the three snipers. He could see their heat and moved the cross hair over a heat signature. A shot rang out from the roof of the barn. A .50 caliber shot. This is the first time that it was fired at a live target. He tapped on another small video and made it bigger he could see another sniper. The tablet monitored about twelve cameras at once. He put the cross hair on the red heat signature and tapped the fire button and another shot rang out. Tech could see the sniper flying off the tree he climbed. He had one left. Tech searched around from video to video, and he spotted something or someone it looked too small. He squinted and decided it was a racoon. He laughed and continued to scan, when he scanned higher up, he saw him. Cross hairs on target and another shot rang out.

"That makes three," Tech was done.

Later back in the house, Jake was checking his email. D.C. Had sent him a large attachment. Jake opened it and started reading, what he saw made him slump down in his chair, "This family is based in Argentina, their whole family is down there running things. This is bigger than I thought," Jake was a little taken back, you could hear it in his voice, when he was explaining things to June and the guys, "The Argentina government is behind us all the way. They have been trying to take out this mafia family for over a year. Every time they try and send out officers or military the villains start telling them what will happen to their families. The mafia knows the names of the officer's wives and children. Yelling their names, addresses and where they work. Laughing while they yelled. The Officers end up leaving without arresting anyone. The Mafia family has control, and they know how to take advantage," Jake reported.

"Archie and I are going to take a trip down there and scope it out," Jake was trying to create a plan.

"Not without me," Casey hollered.

"Or me," Rusty insisted.

Tech said, "I'm good someone must hold down the home front. June can't do it alone."

Written By
J.R. Wilson

The Adventures of
Jake & Archie

Jake laughed, "Ok, gear up everyone. Except Tech, meet me in the barn in thirty."

Everyone in the barn Jake, Casey, and Rusty were geared up and loaded up into Archie. After saying their goodbyes, they were off. It only took Archie a few minutes and they were over the coke processing labs according to the maps Archie downloaded from the emails D.C. had sent.

"If these are the labs, according to these maps. That makes the warehouse twenty miles North of here," Jake was thinking, "Let's head North and find this warehouse," Jake instructed.

After a short trip Archie informed the group, "I believe we're over it Jake?"

"Set down behind those trees Archie," Jake pointed where he wanted Archie to park. Once on the ground the men knew what to do, they split up and surveyed around the outside of the building. No cameras, one guard in the front, he was half asleep. It was late so no one was around. The team got back into Archie, "Let's head to town. I want to see what's going on there."

As they flew over a small village, they could see villagers and some uniformed individuals. They weren't military, they were private security, like the half-asleep guard in front of the warehouse.

"Hmmm, not much resistance, if we were to just walk in. We could level this place, but we don't want to hurt villagers," Jake was sizing up the situation, "You know, I am very proud of how we took down those Ukrainians. Except for the snipers, no bloodshed. We planned and executed. Plus, none of us were injured. I would like to destroy all this stuff! But we must accomplish our mission, and hopefully none of us get hurt. The only ones hurt, should be their lame ass security."

Written By
J.R. Wilson

The Adventures of
Jake & Archie

Casey and Rusty just looked at each other. Sitting in the back seat they were whispering, "Jake was never worried we would get hurt, we would just go in guns a blazing,"
Casey continues, "Maybe he thinks we're getting too old for this kind of action?"

Rusty taps Jake on the shoulder, "Hey boss!"

"What's up," Jake replied.

"You think we're getting too old for this kind of action," asked Rusty.

"What? No! You wouldn't be here if I thought that! Where's this coming from? I was more concerned with over kill, for this little job, but to hell with that, let's just do what we do best," Jake replied.

"Alright, we're going to blow stuff up," said a very enthusiastic Rusty.

"We located their warehouse and labs. Now we need to check out the docks they are controlling," Jake was trying to come up with a plan, where they hit them all at once. He knows he will need some help. Archie had them over the docks and the Ukrainian mobs ship was in. This is a prime opportunity. Maybe he can do this a little differently. Maybe they don't need help after all. Jake throws out a scenario,

"What if we hit the ship and docks hard with Archie? What do you think will happen next."

Casey hated when Jake pop quizzes him, "Everyone will have their attention on the ship," Casey answered.

"Exactly! While they are headed here, we will already be hitting the warehouse. Next to the labs, then we hover outside the mansion and wait for the Leaders to evacuate to a safe house. That's where you guys come in. Firing from Archie might be tricky, you will have to hold real still Archie. We don't want to shoot kids or women; it wouldn't look good. Ya know? I

Written By
J.R. Wilson

figure with Archie we shouldn't be on any of the locations for more than a couple minutes. We should be at the mansion before they start leaving. You guys will have to pick off the leader or generals or anyone who's not a kid or woman...unless they have a gun," Jake laughs, he knows his guys. They do things right and always hit the target.

Just when Jake was going to strike, "What the...? Where? How did we get here Jake," asked Casey.

The Adventures of
Jake & Archie

Chapter 17
Back to the Realm

In an instant they were transported to the realm. The
realm is another way of saying dimensions. It's a realm because
there are magic properties on each planet. Some good some not
so good.

"I have no idea; did you do this Archie," Jake asked.

"No Jake, I'm still figuring out how this happened.
Somehow my portal was pulled open, and we were sucked
through it, but how," Archie seemed confused and that should
never happen.

"Let's set down by the house," Jake was going to
continue, then he saw something he couldn't believe, "Do you
guys see this," Jake said almost to freaked out to speak, cause
Casey and Rusty were too freaked out to speak.

Note: Men like Jake, Casey, Rusty, and Tech don't get
scared. At least they don't talk about it. They get freaked out or
'blown away' or they just make light of... or make fun of what
we would call 'scary'. But they never say scared... so you
know.

What they saw was the commander and his men. They
were alive. Jake used Archie's loudspeaker, "How the hell are

Written By
J.R. Wilson

y'all alive?" Jake yelled. Then he got out of the car. Jake was
armed and the guys had their rifles trained on these weird little
aliens. Who die and come back. *Ha! Sounds like a Bruce Willis
movie*, "Explain before we make you dead again," Then Jake
spoke in a whisper so only Archie could hear," Can you target
all seven of them at once."

"Not a problem I got 'em," Archie came across in Jakes
ear pods.

"Okay, when I give the word, you light them up." Jake
whispered.

The commander in a smug and arrogant tone, "How are
you, Jake. Good to see you."

"Okay, enough, did you bring us here?" Jake was getting
pissed now, he hates leaving work incomplete.

"Yes, my little device here, I had to repair it because
when you shot me, you hit it as well. It was only good for one
transport. All I could think of is bringing you here, so we would
both be stuck here," said the commander in a smug tone.

"SO HOW ARE YOU ALIVE? A fair question and I'm
getting tired of waiting for an answer," Jake was gearing up to
put these alien pricks back to sleep.

"You can't die in this realm; didn't I tell you that? There's
no dying here, you die, and the realm brings you back, better
than ever," the commander is enjoying this.

"How long?" Jake asked.

"How long, how long what?" the commander replied.

"How long before your alive again?" Jake annoyingly
clarified.

"Ooh," said the commander," About Twenty to thirty
minutes, it's absolutely, amazing. Now we are all stuck here, and
we can kill each other, over, and over again,"

Written By
J.R. Wilson

The Adventures of
Jake & Archie

While the commander was talking. Jake remembered when they were looking for the scientists, and they had built a fire. The wood never burned through, hours later the fire was still going strong and looked the same as when they started it. Even putting it out was a chore, dirt wouldn't do it. The fire burned right through. Two full buckets of water did the job. I guess fire is alive, but that old fire and water thing, fire lost.

"Okay Archie, WORD," Jake said out loud. Archie hesitated.

"Oh! WORD is the word," Archie opened up, firing a new looking laser a hard loud beam seven of them, no pulse just WHAM! About six inches in diameter, made a nice hole. Down went the commander and his six commandos. *Commando huh! That's giving them way too much credit.*

Jake hollers at Casey and Rusty, "Body bags we got twenty to thirty minutes to get them out of here. Or we're going to have to do this again."

"Copy that boss," Casey remarked, "How do we get out of here without Archie's portal."

"Not to worry, we will use the same one the scientists used. The cave that takes us to the opposite side of the alien planet. The scientists built a house they never lived in; it was a decoy. They used it for supplies," Jake told the guys.

"Now.... Let's see... how do we load seven body bags into Archie... Aah! Three in the trunk, and four on the hood we bungee them," Jake was laughing at his idea, "It's a short drive through the cave. Then we dump um at the house and have the Amorlites deal with it."

As they approach the cave, Jake asked Archie, "Have you got back your portal door."

Written By
J.R. Wilson

105

The Adventures of
Jake & Archie

"No," Archie said sharply. He seemed extremely concerned, "I'm extremely concerned! It should have reset itself. I'm its home address; this is where it belongs."

As they passed through the tunnel at about the halfway point, they entered the portal it took a couple seconds, and they were out.

Archie announced, "It's back! It's back! It's really, back," Archie was so excited, "My portal door is back," Then he lowered his voice and softly said, "The portal in the cave is gone."

"What's that mean?" Jake wondered out loud.

"It means that portal had the same signature as mine and when we went through. The cave portal grabbed the vacancy. That's the only thing that makes sense," Archie paused briefly, "hypothetically. It's the only theory that makes sense to me."

That was good enough for Jake. They dropped off the ugly seven at the house and hung around, till the Amorlites showed up. The Amorlites took the bodies and before they left. One of them said, "We're going to torch these vermin."

Jake and the guys were ready to get home.

A little more about the realm. This is a place outside our universe. The Amorlites discovered the realm, it is nothing like anything in our universe. The realm is only accessible through Archie's portal. There are twenty planets in the realm. This is the only healing planet. Some of the others are very dangerous. Some have poisoned water or no oxygen. Others have deadly vegetation or massive beasts that are carnivores. Basically, the planet they access in the realm through Archie is the only friendly and safe planet in that galaxy.

"Jake it's a three-hour ride. Tell us something we don't know about you," Rusty liked stories.

Written By
J.R. Wilson

The Adventures of
Jake & Archie

"Let's see… did I ever tell y'all about my first day I could legally hunt?" Jake asked.

"No," Casey said. He was now interested.

"Well… before I was twelve, I couldn't legally hunt. So… I was a bird dog, the dogs would be working in the ditch full of toolies and so did I. When I turned twelve, I went to hunters' safety course. They teach and train valuable information, and it stays with you. Where your barrel is always pointed. How to cross a fence safely stuff like that. So, on the opening day, Dad and I and a couple of his hunting buddies were standing around. Dad bought me a brand new .410 shotgun, double barrel. The men are over at the pickup truck having coffee with a little Baileys. So, I have my shotgun open laying across my arm, that's as safe as you can be, shells showing. Anyway, I'm standing there alone looking around and about forty-five feet from me is a rooster pheasant. He's crouched down in some weeds. I'm the only one who sees him. I'm waiting for the time to start hunting, it's always an odd time 8:03, 8:05 or 8:07 instead of just 8:00.

Dad says, "I got 8:07 you guys," They confirmed. So, I don't say a word. I just close my double barrel raised it up, take aim and… POW! Man, those guys went nuts!"

"What the hell Jake, just because its hunting time doesn't mean just start shooting,"
my dad's friends started into me. Then they started in on Dad, "What did you teach that boy," Dad was just watching me. I didn't turn around to make excuses I just walked over and picked up my bird tagged it. Back then we had ten tags, and that's your limit for the season. I looked over at everyone.

"Got my first bird," I said, holding the animal up. There was a long pause. Looks between the men and then they started

Written By
J.R. Wilson

laughing. They were laughing so hard they had trouble talking to me, it was funny.

"Did... you...see," my dad's friend was wheezing while he was trying to talk,
"that bird… the whole time."

I just nodded and walked into the field to start the hunt. I shot three more birds all were on the rise flying. At the end I had four birds and fired four times, no misses. The men had a whole new respect for me... I think my dad did to," Jake finished his story.

"Great story Jake. Is it true," Asked Rusty.

"Absolutely you can't make up stuff like that. Plus, it's part of my childhood, you never forget those memories," Jake insisted.

They were coming into earth's orbit, that the military was going to complete the mission. Everyone thought Jake and his men had been killed or captured. They receive a message from NASA. Jerry had left the message. The President wants to meet you on the Q.T. here's a direct line.

"Well! The President wants to meet me on the Q.T.," Jake said out loud. Everyone started to laugh...very hard laughter. They headed to the ranch and set Archie down right in front of the barn. No one saw them," The President wants to see me on the sly," Jake wondered out loud," Feels like a setup," Casey remarked," Yeah it kind of does," Jake agreed. June came out they were all on the Porch," The President wants to see you honey," June was exciting," Yes, he does, but we will do it on my terms. How's the runway looking I haven't been back there in months," "I was just back there checking it out last week," Tech went on," Everything is working. I was going to fill you in, but there was nothing to report. Then we got very busy, and I didn't think to bring it up."

Written By
J.R. Wilson

The Adventures of
Jake & Archie

"Gates are working, tower has power," Jake loves quizzing Tech," Everything is working, when do we need it?" Tech asked.

"Not sure yet. I'll know soon. If this meeting is for real," Jake mumbled, "Let's call and find out."

"Tech calls the number put it on speaker," Jake was very official sounding.

The party at the other end answered, "This is the President, is this Jake?"

Jake answered, "Yes sir, this is Jake, what can I do for you sir?"

"We need to meet, but in secret," The President sounded nervous.

"Well, you can land here at my ranch it's got a mile, and a half runway have your pilot call, and we will give him all the info he needs. The runway is well lit and deep inside my property no one can get near, there are over fifty cameras covering the whole area,"

"That's a great idea my secret service will want six or more agents with me is that going to be a problem," The President seems more upbeat.

"Not for me, just give me an approximate time and we will be ready. If your secret service wants to come ahead of time no problem they can run amuck," Jake kind a chuckled.

"Are they really coming here," June asked.

"You were right here, you heard what I heard, so I guess we will see," Jake is trying to sound casual. I have a feeling that he wants us to perform a mission, and I think I know what and where. Jake was thinking.

Jake received a call from the pilot, a video call. Jake liked it because he could see the guy and behind him was the President. It really puts his mind at ease. Jake gave all the flight

Written By
J.R. Wilson

109

information, GPS, and landing assistance to the pilot," There
will be secret service at your ranch in the morning," The pilot
informed Jake. Jake was fine with that.

The Adventures of
Jake & Archie

Chapter 18
The President Takes a Ride

The secret service wasn't very secret. Jake was watching, "Man, these guys really do run amuck. Tech is in with one of the agents, showing him our security system. I'm going out to the runway," June handed Jake a cup of coffee and a little kiss. He headed to the barn.

"Archie let's take a drive out to the runway," Jake said while climbing into the car.

"I'll drive," Jake instructed.

They drove out and it was a beautiful day. Jake remarked, "Nothing like being in Colorado on a sunny day like today," Archie pulled up to the control tower. The tower was stacked with six small modular homes. They were stacked two side by side, then two on top making a cross then two more on top making it cross again. They put a stairway in the middle of the structure. The building has lots of windows so you can see out wherever you stand.

Jake's dad had the runway built when he was getting on in years. He always liked this spot because the land was very level. Jake and his mom didn't mind; it kept his dad busy. After a couple of years and five million dollars the runway and the

Written By
J.R. Wilson

tower were complete. Jake's dad believed they would need it because the future is coming fast, and he thought it would be necessary for the town and for the family.

Jake got out of Archie. There was a secret service agent standing there, "What the hell, you have closed gates across the runway six of them," The agent complained.

"Good morning to you…" Jake said greeting the agent, "Come inside and we will fix the gates being closed. We have gates to keep unwanted guests from landing here," Jake turned a few switches and all the gates open, "See no big deal. When is the President getting here," Jake was curious. The agent ignored him when he saw the gates open, he just went back downstairs. Jake stood there thinking, *these guys never change, he better be good at his job. Oh well, let it go.*

About three hours later Air Force One was calling. Jake answered, gave them the local info on the runway and wind directions cleared them to land. They called back and spoke.

"We're on final approach," Watching that big aircraft coming in was something.
It's so BIG! How can it fly? But Air Force One set down just as smooth as silk. All this is running through Jakes head. *Meeting the President why am I thinking of all this stupid stuff? Calm down, remember what you want to say, stick to your plan, it will all work fine.*

Jake gets in Archie and pulls up to the massive jet. He parks alongside the steps. Then Jake gets out of Archie.

The President appears in the door, "Hello Jake, nice to finally meet you in person."

"Yes sir, Mr. President. This is a thrill for me," Jake was back. No more nervous stupid thoughts. He had a plan and was on the job.

Written By
J.R. Wilson   112

The Adventures of
Jake & Archie

"That is one big jet, Mr. President," Jake was dangling the bait.

"Oh, well come in take a look we can talk in here," The President offered. Jake is thinking. Hook, line, and sinker, I landed a big one. When Jake arrived at the top of the steps and walked inside Air Force One.

He was totally blown away, "This is great sir, wow! Oh, hey there's something I must do. Where's the head sir."

The President laughed, "Ok, you need to lower your float? There's a couple of them. One is up on your left."

Jake ducked in and grabbed a hand towel with the Presidential seal on it, "No sir, I just wanted the towel for my wife to frame."

The President laughs "So… you're stealing from Air Force One?"

"I'll pay you for it," Jake tells him.

The President says, "Everyone comes on board and steals from this plane, you're the first to declare it and be so direct," He was still laughing.

"Mr. President, can I ask a small favor," asked Jake, "Would you sign the towel."

"Sure," The President agrees with a smile. So, using a marker the President signs the towel.

"Alright," said Jake.

"One day this towel will be worth a lot more than this fancy jet,"

"Why," Said the President, "Because I signed it."

"Well yeah, that's part of it. You see, that's the first thing you signed in office, using only one pen."

The President just got this blank look on his face, he looked at Jake and looked around the room at everyone like he

Written By
J.R. Wilson   113

was standing in his underwater, in front of everyone. Then he started to laugh and said, "You got me Jake."

They finally sit down, everyone else leaves the room. It's just Jake and President.

Archie whispers to Jake in his ear pods, "There are three bugs in that room you want me to disable them."

"Not yet," replied Jake.

"Hey sir, did you know there are at least three bugs in this room," Jake declared.

"There is? How do you know that?" The President really looked surprised, but it's hard to tell if he is surprised about the bugs, or if he's surprised Jake knew about them.

"Archie scanned the plane. He always has my back sir," Jake said proudly.

"Archie is that the car," the commander and chief asks.

"Yes sir," Jake acknowledged.

"Tell me more about your car," asked the commander and chief.

Jake starts telling him the story, a snapshot version of how he and Archie met.

"Wow! That's something, maybe we should impound it for our own purposes,"
The President was testing the waters. Jake laughed," You can try and try and even try some more."

"It will never work we are linked he won't operate for anyone but me."

"I was kidding I understand not to break up a great team."

The President went on," I need you for a mission. Also, from time to time I want to call on you."

"I see is that maybe, Argentina, Ukrainian mafia," Jake guessed.

Written By
J.R. Wilson

The Adventures of
Jake & Archie

"You know about that? You know about the mission you know about the bugs on my plane."

The President goes to the door that leads to a bigger room with agents and advisors.

Opens it and yells, "Whose running security around here."

Jake laughs and says "You need to understand. You don't ever lie to me. If you do, I will find out, I always do."

"I won't lie to you. If you lie to me, that's it, you will never get my services again. So just tell me the truth it's doesn't matter to me if is horrible or crazy weird, we can deal with it. I don't judge. Well not often." He chuckled.

"The three reasons for my help," Jake went on, "One: Personal. Two; Professional, trying to save your job. Three; a threat to our country or our planet."

"One of these three I will help, can you guess which one?"

Jake made things clear, "In ten years, you will be gone. I will still be me, and the next President will want my help,"

"Oh no," proclaimed the President, "I will have you working for me," Jake laughed.

"No that will never happen, sorry."

"I will pay you what an athlete makes. Thirty million a year salary, ten million for insurance. That's a lot of money."

"I already have a lot of money," Jake declared "I don't need your money okay."

"Let me tell you about the sheik," Jake goes on to tell the President all about the Shiek, everything.

President wanted to know whatever happened to that sheik.

Jake just turned to the President and said in a very cold manner, "I killed him. Pushed him out of a helicopter,"

Written By
J.R. Wilson

The Adventures of
Jake & Archie

The President didn't flinch. He knew how to stay unreadable, "How about a ride in your car, Jake?"

"Sure, why not," Jake just landed the big fish.

So, they load up in Archie. The secret service agents were giving birth to a set of dishes! They were wigging out!

"Sir you can't just go for a ride with him," one of them said.

"Sure, I can. If Obama can go for a ride with Seinfeld. I can ride in the safest vehicle on the planet," He looked at Jake, "Isn't that right?"

Jake said, "It sure is."

"Look if one or two of you want to come it's fine with me," Jake didn't care, he knew what the President would say," No, just you and me, we have things to discuss."

The agents didn't like it, but before they could do anything. Archie took off down the runway. The agents didn't follow, after all they were on a runway in the country, there was nowhere to go.

Archie was just about to the end of the runway. The President looked over at Jake a bit worried. Archie took off and the agents couldn't see him anymore.

"Go to stealth, please and I will hit the green button, and you know where to go, pal."

Jake looked at the President and reassured him it was all good. "We are flying! We are flying very fast! Yet I don't feel the speed or the turns," The President was having trouble processing all this.

"That's the green button it is an inertia suppressor. I know! We still haven't figured out a good name for it," Jake excused himself. Within a few minutes they were over the docks.

Written By
J.R. Wilson

116

The Adventures of
Jake & Archie

"Do you know what this is Mr. President? It's the Ukrainian's dock and one of their warehouses. Go ahead Archie do your thing."

Jake was giving the President a tour and at the same time taking out the Ukrainians distribution and manufacturing. Archie fired several times at the water line of the ship. The ship was sinking. Archie blew up the dock and the storage facility.

"Good deal Archie. Next," Archie headed for the next stop. Another warehouse and Archie went to work and blew it sky high. The President could hardly believe what he's seeing. Next, they were off to the fields. Archie has three locations where they process coke. Jake was still looking for a meth lab. When Archie swooped down and targeted the coke processing huts, he hit one after another. Up in flames. They were making their turn around and Archie pick up a signal, "Ten degrees to port Jake! I think we found their meth lab."

Jake and the President looked and in the trees, they could see smoke and big canvas tents. Archie scanned the tent and it's a meth lab. A couple of quick shots and BOOM! No more meth lab.

"Take us to the runway Archie our work here is done," Jake smiled over at the President, and he was doing the bugged eyed thing with his jaw hanging down.

"You ever hang out with my crew, y'all have a lot in common," Jake laughed.
In a few minutes they were over the ranch.

"First land in front of the house, June will be pissed if she doesn't get to meet you sir," Jake said to the President.

"That's fine! We are way ahead of the game. I didn't realize we would run the mission on our little drive. Now we got time to kill," President was gleaming.

Written By
J.R. Wilson

The Adventures of
Jake & Archie

"I must warn you. There's probably a feast southern style in the house. June will want you to eat and more than likely have a doggy bag for you," Jake cautioned.

"Wonderful I'm hungry aren't you," Said the President, "Great come in and meet my better half," Jake was proud of his family.

When they entered the house Bullet was lying there. He looked up at The President then stood up. Then his lip started to quiver, and a low deep growl was building. Jake saw what was happening and told Bullet.

"It's okay boy, he's a friend, its fine," Bullet turned and walked into the kitchen. He kept an eye on the President on the way to the kitchen, "Don't worry sir, he won't bother you, he's a good dog. He will know you next time you come here," *funny*, Jake was thinking, *Bullet has always been a good judge of persons character and human nature.*

June came out of the kitchen and found the two fellas sitting in the living room. She walked up to the President, who stood up to greet her. She curtsied. Jake introduced, "This my wife June. June says hello to our President. You don't curtsy for the President; he's not a king," Jake laughed.

June gave Jake a smack crossed his chest, "Hello Mr. President it's a great pleasure to meet you sir," June was busting at the seams she was so excited.

"I hope you're hungry," June said, "We have pulled pork with Carolina BBQ sauce, corn on the cobb, sweet potato crunch, popcorn shrimp, some ribs we slow cooked all day. The pulled pork is a pig we buried in hot embers all night and it is tender and don't forget the yeast rolls. Here's some sweet tea," The President and Jake dived right in, not much talking just a whole lot of chewing.

Written By
J.R. Wilson

The Adventures of
Jake & Archie

As they finished up June brought out a doggy bag for the President. She also gave Jake eight made-up plates for the secret service agents back at the plane.

When they were ready to head to the plane Jake had an idea, "Sir you want to have some fun with your agents."

"What did you have in mind?"

"We'll stay stealth we will fly over the plane and Archie can beat you into Air Force One."

"He can do that," The President asked.

"Not a problem," Archie said, "I can beat you, to your bedroom. It will drive them crazy how you managed to get on the plane without them seeing you."

"Okay beam away… it won't hurt will it," President was a little worried, "Nope you won't feel a thing," Archie reassured him.

"One more thing I need to say. When I said. No personal reason. I meant personal gain or getting you out of a mess you made. If something happens with a family member or someone is hunting you, of course we will help if we can. We good Mr. President," Jake hoped they were good," We're Good," With a flash the President was gone. Archie landed and turned off the stealth. Jake pulled up, and the agents walked over. Opened the passenger door.

"Where's the President, oh crap! What happened to him," The agent was panicking.
Jake pointed it out," Look up at the door."

They looked and there stood the President waving at them.

"What the hell! How did he get there," An agent asked.

They were all looking at Jake. He just smiled and said, "Magic."

Written By
J.R. Wilson

The Adventures of
Jake & Archie

You know, if you think about it, that's not far from the truth. Jake pulled over to the tower and went in to see the President off. He scanned the skies for air traffic," Air Force One you're all clear for takeoff," The huge jet went down the runway and at the last moment.
it lifted off. Jake got on radio and said his, goodbyes and stay safe. They responded, "thank you, it was an enjoyable visit."

Jake went back to the house and had dessert, and hot rum toddies with June , yes they were back on the porch.

June spoke," You and I always enjoy our quiet time out here. It's weird that all this stuff started right here," Jake laughed, "Yep it all started here, but we certainly got to see some sights."

"I think tomorrow night we should go out for dinner," Offered Jake," Oh wonderful going out to eat twice in one day," June liked the idea.

"Twice what do you mean," Jake asked, "Well tomorrow is Saturday, and we usually go to breakfast in town at the cafe," June reminded Jake.

"Oh yea, I forgot well the hell with dinner," Jake was messing with June.

"Oh no you don't, you said we go somewhere nice," June insisted.

Jake was laughing," I'm just messing with you; we will do both. With Archies help we. Can have dinner anywhere in the world you want."

"Even Paris or somewhere in Italy," June questioned.

"Of course, anywhere," Jake gave his word, "I promise."

Written By
J.R. Wilson

Chapter 19
Jake and June go to Town

The next morning Jake and June load up into Archie,
"Where to Jake… or should I ask June."
June answered, "We're going to the café in town Archie
boy."
They took off and when they got to the edge of town
Archie found a quiet road, no one around. He landed on the road
and turns off the stealth. They pulled up to the café and like
every Saturday it's packed. June and Jake Walk in, and June's
other sister Susan greeted them, and she put them in her own sec
"Coffee," Susan asked.
While she was getting them coffee, they were deciding
on what to have. Susan returned with their coffee," Do you
know what you want Sis," June ordered. A Denver omelet, hash
browns, sour dough toast. Jake ordered biscuits and gravy, hash
browns, a couple links three eggs scrambled soft.
"Best biscuits and gravy in Colorado," Jake declared.
"You say that every time we eat here. I swear you would
eat biscuits and gravy for breakfast, lunch, and dinner," June
was teasing.
"Yeah… what's your point," Jake agreed.

Written By
J.R. Wilson

The Adventures of
Jake & Archie

"Hi, ya Jake, how ya doing brother," Jake turned around and it was an old friend; they had gone on missions together for close to ten years.

"Hey Sam, good to see you everything working for you," Jake was very happy to see Sam they were good friends back in the day.

"Yes, the wife and I moved here a few days ago. The guys in our squad won't stop talking about this place. My tour was up. We figured this is the place to be. I'm glad I ran into you."

"This is great. Do you need help moving in? The guys I would love to help," Jake inquired.

"Nah we're down to emptying boxes, the movers got it done fast," Sam always had things under control. That's one of the reasons Jake liked him, he is one solid individual. You could aways count on him.

Food arrives. Jake says, "Sam you and your better half grab your plates and join us,"

"Sure enough, thank you," Sam was very excited because he ran into Jake. If he hadn't, the next day he was going to hunt him down. Jake was the reason Sam moved here. He knew if Jake was here, it is the place to be.

"Why don't you two come for dinner tomorrow night around six o'clock," Jake invited them so he could talk with Sam in private.

"That's a date," Proclaimed Sam.

Sam introduced his wife," This is Terri," They all talked and ate," This place has excellent food," Sam was really pigging out.

Terri said, "This is really good food unusual for a café. They are usually kind of greasy but not here this place must have a real chef."

Written By
J.R. Wilson

The Adventures of
Jake & Archie

"The cook is a chef his specialty is steaks, and he does wonderful things with potatoes," Jake was bragging with his mouth full of biscuits.

After their meal Jake and June followed Sam and Terri to their new house.

"When did you get that Maserati," Sam Asked, "That car is sweet."

"Oh, it's a long story, maybe one day I will tell you all about it," Jake wanted to tell him everything. But it was too soon.

When the time is right Jake will know. Jake was thinking about what happened to Vicki. Sam and Vicki were together for eight years. When Jake retired, he had lost touch with Sam, I guess people break up every day, oh well.

June and Terri were in the kitchen, "This is a lovely home I'm very impressed with what two have done so far," June continued, "I know Jake is so happy Sam is here. I hope we can be friends, if you need anything. You call me, you have friends here."

"Thank you," Terri was feeling a little less pressure, June talking with her loosened Terri up a bit.

"You are coming for dinner tomorrow, aren't you," June wanted a guarantee.

"Of course I can't wait to see your ranch. Do you have horses?"

"We have six horses left and about a hundred head of white face cattle. Come out a little earlier and we can go for a ride," June offered thinking it might make them closer.

"That would be outstanding, I can't wait," Terri seemed truly excited.

Written By
J.R. Wilson

The Adventures of
Jake & Archie

Jake and Sam were looking at Archie, "This is a beautiful car," Sam pointed out, "It must have cost you a bundle."

"Oh, I got a pretty good deal," Jake didn't know what else to say," You guys come out to the ranch earlier tomorrow I'm sure we will find something to do," Jake chuckled.
Jake and June visited for a while longer and soon they were headed home," I liked her," June said, "She seems strong and nice."

"Yeah, she does. You remember me talking about Sam when we deployed to Iraq," Jake mentioned.

"Of course, it just seems so long ago," June said, "You guys did a lot over there,"
That night Jake and June were getting ready to go out for dinner.

"Where do you want to go June."

"I don't know the good restaurants in Paris or Italy, why don't we go to Denver I like that place, that has the first alcohol issued in Colorado. It's number one. Their steaks are unbelievably great."

"You are reading my mind," Jake stated. Archie took them into Denver. The next day was Sunday and Archie wanted to check out some readings he is receiving.

"Jake, you got your ear pods in," Archie wanted to talk to Jake badly.

"Sure do! What's up Archie."

"Can you come out to the barn for a quick talk."
Jake said, "Ok be right there."
In the barn Jake sat down in front of Archie.

"Ok what's going on," Jake was in a good mood because of Sam living in town, he had another friend close by.

Written By
J.R. Wilson

The Adventures of
Jake & Archie

"We have some company, or we are about to have some company," Archie continued, "Theres a fleet coming towards earth, I think NASA knows cause Jerry's been texting."

"Text him back tell him we're headed out," Jake instructed.

"Yes sir, on it," Archie obeyed.

About that time, Sam and Terri showed up, Jake or maybe June, one of them last night, told Terri to come out early for some horseback riding. Jake hollered at the guys to help out with the horses.

June came out to greet Sam and Terri, "Good morning, you want to come in for some coffee? While the guys get the horses saddled up."

"Sure," Sam responded. Sam is a big guy, African American, built like he was born in a weight room. A little over six feet. Letting his hair grow out. Jake liked how he always had Jakes back in a fight and Jake always had his. From the first day they met, they were instantly friends. Terri is Spanish or Cuban. About five foot four inches good body rather athletic.

"Sam! Come into the living room," Jake requested. They both grabbed their coffee.

"Um, Sam I have a problem something just came up and I have to move on this now. I'm sure the guys and June can take you riding. I got to go."

"What is it can I help," Sam offered.

"If your serious it could get a little freaky," Jake warned.

"Hell yeah, some action would do me some good, and being with you it will be like old times," Sam was excited. In the barn Jake supplied some gear vest, side arm, rifle.

Written By
J.R. Wilson

Chapter 20
Another Invasion and Rescue

"Where we are going Jake," asked Archie.

"Oh, you will see, load up into Archie," said Jake.

"Archie? Since when do, you name your car," Sam got a chuckle out of that.

As they backed out and drove down the driveway. Jake tells Archie, "Wait till we are alone on the county road."

"Understood," Archie replied.

"Wait a damn minute. Your car and you talk to each other, and wait for what," Sam wanted to know what's the plan."

"Yes Sam... Archie and I talk. He isn't just a car he is alive and capable of doing extraordinary things you'll see."

"Don't look at me like that. Have I ever lied to you...ever," Jake said very seriously.

"Archie, it looks clear. Stealth up and get us there quick," Jake snapped.

Archie was quick bam stealth, bam, their headed towards outer space. Sam was staring at Jake. Yes, he too had bug eyes and jaw dropping. Jake said," It's okay, this is just another day for Archie and me. We are headed out to see what an invasion fleet is coming to earth. We are going to evaluate the situation."

Written By
J.R. Wilson

The Adventures of
Jake & Archie

"Invasion fleet coming to earth? This is how you spend your Sunday," Sam laughed nervously.

"We will see, this is an unknown alien. I'm interested in their intentions. Take us in for a closer look," Jake was wanting to see how big the fleet is.

"Wow," Jake was shocked, "look how big those ships are, their very big I mean BIG, WAY BIG! SOOO BIG! Dang-O!"

Sam just got worried, "Ahhh… do you think this is bigger than you anticipated," Just asking," This is all new for me what do you think."

"It's okay Sam, Archie can you hear anything, are they transmitting."

"Yes sir. Their transmitting. How they are going to rule our galaxy," Archie reported.

"Let me hear them, can you translate," Jake asked.

"Rule the galaxy," Sam said," What happened to ruling the planet."

"They are obviously hostile. Archie, see what your cannons can do to that BIG, BIG, BIG SHIP."

Archie let loose with his laser canons, and the aliens force field was too thick the cannons were just ricocheting off. *Hmmm that sucks,* thought Jake.

"They're firing at us."

"What? Can they see us," Jake was starting to worry now.

"I can only think of one reason they see us. They are using a system that they fill an area with micro particles so when we pass through them, they see our path," Archie informed them.

"Archie swings out wide, come in behind and above their ships. I want to line up on their engines," Jake ordered.

Written By
J.R. Wilson   127

The Adventures of
Jake & Archie

"That laser you used on the commander and his men fire that puppy right into their engines. That's got to be the thinnest part of the field," Jake hoped.

Archie widened the beam from six inches to about ten inches. Then he poured as much power he could into firing that laser, it went in. Then out the other end of the ship when the beam hit the inside of the force field it spread around the ship and just imploded the ship. Before Jake could react. Archie maneuvers around behind the other two ships and repeats the process and all three ships were in pieces.

Jake and Sam just looked at each other. Just like it was on que both men reached out and patted Archie's dash and said.

"Good... Good boy Archie you're a good boy and did an outstanding job," A Smile appeared on the screen on Archie's dash.

Mean time back in the kitchen June was getting tired of twenty questions. June saw a bulge on Terri's lower back. She was pretty sure it wasn't a back brace. She was trying to remember where Jake's pistol hiding places were. Then it hit her, she was near one under the kitchen counter. Terri was pretty sure June was on to her. She kept thinking about the *damn cheap ring*. She thought it gave her away. The ring was part of it, but it was the questions they gave her up.

Plus, not once did she talk about Sam or was even curious why they were gone or where they went. When Terri went for her gun tucked in her back. June just reached under the counter it was aiming at Terri at the end of the counter. These hidden guns are loaded, cocked and ready to shoot. So, June just pulled the trigger, when Terri swung her weapon around June

Written By
J.R. Wilson

128

had already fired. It hit Terri right in the gut. June pulled the gun out from under the counter. Terri was raising up to shoot; she wasn't quitting yet. June just aimed and fired three more rounds and the was the end of Terri.

June realized why Jake had put a suppressor on the house guns. It was quiet and she didn't even need ear plugs, like they use on the range, "Bitch you're getting blood on my clean kitchen floor," June grabbed the intercom and called Casey and the guys. They came running. When they walked in the kitchen that's when they got upset.

"Oh fine, even June is getting more action then us. I thought we were supposed to kill folks! Jake and June are having all the fun," Rusty complained. Casey and Tech laughed. They were trying to relax June; she is getting keyed up.

"Let's get the bitch rolled up in a tarp. I'll get the shop vac," said Tech.

"What do I tell Sam," June worried.

"It's okay we will deal with this; you just go in sit down and take it easy," Casey walked her into the living room, made her a strong drink. June just put her head back and closed her eyes.

This had a bigger impact on June than she thought. She dosed off.

"Archie you still monitoring."

"Yes, I am. I have something interesting. Listen to this," They could hear a conversation after it was run through Archie's interpreter. They made mention of a woman being held. That's the Ukrainian mafia.

"Archie, can you narrow that down and give us a location," Jake figured two birds with one Archie. Archie brought them into orbit.

That's when NASA was calling, "Jake you there?"

Written By
J.R. Wilson

The Adventures of
Jake & Archie

"Yea Jerry, we are fine, however that fleet, not friendly at all. We changed their mind," Jake laughed.

"Look we have something to do I'll holler back at you later."

"Where to Archie?"

"The city, it's coming from a high-income area Jake."

"Sounds good, we get to wake up some rich folks," Jake is trying to stay loose.

"Sam you ready to get Vicki back," Jake was stoking the fire.

"You just tell me what to do Jake," Sam was fired up.

"Archie has a location so we're going to recon the area first. Hopefully, Archie will locate Vicki. Then we go in while Archie shoots the crap out of the other end of the house. The distraction should help," Jake was pretty sure it should work.

Sam wanted to know," Jake are we shooting anyone who gets in our way?

"Why do you think we have suppressors," Jake was wanting to get as many as possible. That's less of them that can attack his ranch. Archie slid up to the house as close as he could get, still in stealth mode. Jake and Sam had to crawl out of the side windows the car was so close the doors wouldn't open. They kept their backs against the wall, no cameras, even if there were cameras Archie would make short work of them. They found her room and were waiting for Archie to strike. Soon all hell broke loose Archie was blowing stuff up. Along with half the house. Sam and Jake slipped in through a window. Sam went for Vicki and Jake kept WATCHIG THEIR BACKS. Once Sam had Vicki Jake called Archie in for a pickup. When Vicki saw the door open, she passed out, more from hunger then from shock of an invisible car door opening.

Written By
J.R. Wilson

The Adventures of
Jake & Archie

Once they were on board, "Jake aren't we going to take out those pricks," Sam wanted some payback.

Jake said, "Of course we are just turning into position, so we get clean shots. Archie how many left?"

Archie had six heat signatures, "Can you hit them from here."

Jake was hoping he could. Archie fired six laser beams and that was that. The house burst into flames and Archie flew off for the ranch.

"That was easy," Sam commented," Archie did most of it, thank you Archie and thank you Jake, you really got me out of a sticky situation."

"How did you get involved with those jackasses," Jake asked, "I don't know somehow they knew all about me and the fact you and I are friends."

"Huh, I think I need to talk to my guy in D.C," Jake was trying to understand how the Ukrainians could put Sam and Jake as pals.

"We might have a leak somewhere. I don't think it's at our end. Instead of calling I believe I will make this a personal visit," Jake was telling Sam.

"Sounds good, I wouldn't mind getting in on that, you want some company," Sam wanted to know who is messing with his life.

"You're always welcome Sam."

As they were landing at the ranch. Jake could sense something wasn't right. When Jake and Sam were getting out of Archie. Sam told Vicki to wait a minute in the car. They both were armed and approaching the house very cautiously. When Casey came to the door Jake first thought, "Is June okay? What's going on Casey."

Written By
J.R. Wilson

The Adventures of
Jake & Archie

"Relax you missed the fun. Heck, we missed the fun. June took care of everything," Casey bragged," She's sleeping so, keep it down she had a rough time."

"Tell me what happened," while Casey was filling in Jake. Sam was getting Vicki out of the car and ask Jake, "Is there someplace…"

Jake interrupted," Yea, there's a bedroom on your right, make yourself at home, it has a bathroom, towels are in there."

"Okay, Great thank you," Sam knew Vicki needed some rest.

"Jake was sitting with June as she slept," Tech looked in and saw Jake in the living room with June. He gave a hand signal to Jake to join him in the kitchen. Jake came in and asked Tech, "What the hell went on here."

"Let's see, we came in after June called us," Tech went on to tell Jake everything he knew. Jake was upset he had a feeling about Terri, He felt like it was his fault leaving June alone with someone he really didn't know.

"I guess my hidden pistols weren't a bad idea," Jake remarked.

"Saved June that's for sure," Tech agreed.

"Do you think we will have any more trouble from the Ukrainians," Tech asked," If so, it will only be a few we pretty well wiped out most of them. I guess time will tell," speculated Jake.

"I need some rest, get me up when June wakes up or in a few hours," Jake was bushed.

The next morning June was making coffee and seemed fine after some much needed rest. Jake came in and gave her a hug and asked if she was okay.

"I'm fine," June answered.

Written By
J.R. Wilson

The Adventures of
Jake & Archie

"That was quiet the experience, I'm glad you taught me how to handle a pistol," June continued," Terri got blood all over the kitchen floor and the boys did a great job cleaning it up. She was a sneaky bitch," Sam just walked in and overheard what was being said.

"She was a paid assassin. She was in control, as long as they had Vicki. I wanted to tell you everything, but I was worried about Vicki," Sam didn't know how to thank Jake for all he did.

He gave June a big hug, "June I'm so sorry for all this mess. They found out, somehow that Jake and I were old friends someone high up must have sold us out."

"Don't worry about it we will get to the bottom of this," Jake reassured everyone.

"We are still bros if something like this happens again you tell me right away agreed."

"Agreed," Sam was happy, he knew he was going to be okay with Jake apart of his life again. Sam had confidence the two of them could get through this ordeal.

"I believe we need to go to D.C. and talk to some folks," Jake wanted answers, and he believed. D.C. was a good place to start.

"First y'all need to have some breakfast go sit down and I'm going to be a few minutes," June declared.

"You're a lucky man Jake," Sam said.

"Yeah you should have seen her when the Grullers beamed her up to their ship," Jake was laughing," She grabbed an alien rifle and started shooting up their ship," Still laughing Jake said," They beamed her back down in less than ten minutes."

Sam and Jake were both laughing. Vicki walked in and said, "What's so funny?"

Written By
J.R. Wilson

"Oh, we figure June could hold off an invasion single handed," Sam and Jake were laughing even harder. When Sam and Jake went out to the barn the guys Joined them.

"Let's have a quick meeting gather round here," Jake was coming up with a plan.

"We are going to D.C. we need to find out who sold us out."

"I want all of us to go but after what happened here last night, I need at least two of us to stay behind and keep an eye on things. Any volunteers," Jake didn't want to leave the girls unguarded.

Rusty said, "I'll stay I still have to feed the critters."

"Tech, you want to go. You need to get out," Rusty pointed out.

Casey said, "Works for me I have a couple things around here. I wanted to get done, plus we need to reload our pipe bombs, I have a hunch we may need them again."

"Great that sounds good way to look out and plan ahead," Jake never has to worry about the guys they are always putting the ranch first. Jake should have put them on high alert. When Sam and he left to deal with the invasion fleet. He blames himself for June being put in jeopardy. All he had to do was tell them to hang out in the house, but he didn't, he should have listened to his gut when he met Terri, but he didn't.

Written By
J.R. Wilson

Chapter 21
A Trip to D.C.

"Alright Tech you're with us. Don't forget your handy
little items, anything we can bug or use for surveillance."

"Got you covered," Tech said with confidence.

"Archie how's your surveillance equipment we may need
a few tricks," Jake was wanting all the advantages he could get.
Archie assured him, he had a few things Jake hasn't seen yet.

"Those fellas in D.C. may not like it, do to security. But
we are getting to the bottom of this and we're going to find out
who's selling us out. We know we aren't a security risk, so we
get all we can. Everyone good with that, "Jake laid out his
intentions and he was angry. What happened with June being
put in danger and Sam being brought in under duress? The
kidnapping of Vicki, "This ends today," Jake declared.

The Three of them loaded up into Archie. The headed
off the ranch and straight to D.C. on route Jake requested," We
need to call our guy in D.C. Archie I need you to track the call.
We need to know right where he's located."

Tech was on the phone calling him as per Jake.

"I have him, he wants to talk to you Jake," Tech handed
his phone to Jake.

Written By
J.R. Wilson   135

The Adventures of
Jake & Archie

"Hello, how are ya? We have an issue we want to address. Jake wasn't being subtle; he wanted the voice to know.

"I'm fine, what's got you so fired up Jake."

"I'm coming there, where can we meet," Jake ordered.

"Ok where are you," The voice asked.

"In route be there soon, where can we meet."

"Just come to my office you remember where that is don't you."

Jake wasn't sure it's been a while "Send me a text on this phone with your address."

"You got it," they said. What the voice didn't know is that they were hovering just outside in stealth mode. Archie had a location where the voice was talking from, and it wasn't from the voices office. Tech, we need to bug his office even though he's not there.

"Oh, I got this Jake," Archie interrupted," I can fire a dart into the outside of his window. I can fire a few darts around all these windows."

"Go for it, Archie boy," Jake liked what he's hearing.

"Now where is the voice? Jake asked.

"About a mile from here Jake."

"Well let's get there," Flying in Archie while in stealth can be a problem in D.C. there are a lot of helicopters that fly around without warning, so Archie was having to monitor all flights. When they found the location, it was in a tall office building. Archie was trying to get a fix on exactly where he is.

"Archie set down in the roof we will go in from there. You keep looking and let me know when you get a hit."

"Copy that," Archie obeyed. Archie set down in the roof and the three guys head in through the roof door. While the guys were going down the stairwell, Tech mentioned.

Written By
J.R. Wilson

136

The Adventures of
Jake & Archie

"You know Jake, If he wasn't at his office, then why did he send us there."

"I was thinking the same thing," Sam said. The voice sounds familiar I can't place it... but I will."

"You think he was setting us up," Jake questioned.

"It feels like it was a set up doesn't it," Sam wondered.

"I have that ole funny feeling," Jake said, "My gut is talking to me."

"Jake, I got him. He's on the tenth floor, south end, office at the end of the hall," Archie reported.

"Thanks bud. Keep an eye on us if you can," Jake didn't like this one bit, "How many are in there."

"Three I see three heat signatures," Archie said.

"Ok guys, here's what we do we rush the door no shooting unless they start it. If he's here we grab him and go to the roof. If it's not him then we just leave, those guys won't know what to think," Jake felt good about that.

"Suppressors on, pistols only, we don't need to draw attention going in, coming out doesn't matter," Jake is in assault mode and so are Sam and Tech. As they worked their way down to the tenth floor. Archie came on again, in Jakes ear pods," There are more now, it looks like two more arrived. That makes five and they have weapons,"

"Archie, I need you to blow out their windows they will expect us to repel down; they will be looking for us to come in the window," Jake whispered.

"Copy that boss" Archie whispered back.

"Men we are going to break in when we hear Archie's attack."

"Archie, I need locations where they are when you attack."

"I got you covered," Archie reassured Jake.

Written By
J.R. Wilson

Then all hell broke loose, Archie was telling Jake where the men are located. They busted through the door.

"Two on your left, the rest are at the window, their looking up," Jake took out the two on the left. Sam and Tech took care of the other two which left the voice hiding behind his desk.

"Come out we won't hurt you," Jake ordered. The voice stood up "hey, he was the commanding officer of our squad. You remember him Jake, he dispatched your squad a few times, when you and I would work together."

"Yea I remember him. So, colonel why did you lie to me? You don't lie to me ever. You know this. I always find out," Jake was close to ending this guy," You put my wife in danger, "Who are you really working for."

"Jake, we need to talk," said the colonel.

"Archie come and pick us up this place is going to be covered in firemen and cops; can you pull inside the office you blew a big enough hole," Archie pulled right in, and everyone got aboard. They took off.

"This is amazing, where did you get this car? No wonder you get around everywhere so fast."

"Shut it! All I want to hear from you is the truth. Start telling me about what you have to do with the Ukrainians. You are really close to finding out if you can fly."

"Ok! Ok, take it easy I will tell you everything," The colonel was very nervous.

"Start with, what the hell are you doing and who do you work for."

"I'm still a government employee. I handle missions from my office. My blown-up office. Instead of on government property. I wanted to let you know but the Ukrainian mafia found me and my family. I had to help them I wanted to talk with you directly to fill you in, but you never answer your phone its always Tech."

"Hey, don't put this off on me. Typical government workers always find someone to blame to cover your own ass," Jake has had enough this guy.

"You better do better than that. Or you're going out the door."

"Please don't I will tell you," The colonel was pleading.

"I don't know," Tech said," I think he's full of crap he's not going to tell us anything."

"Let's see if he can fly, we will find out what we need to from other sources," Tech wanted to end this guy.

"Wait I have a plan. Archie takes us to the sheriff's office. We will work on him there; he might know this guy or one of his deputies could also know him," Jake was thinking we have to break him. Tech called ahead to the sheriff and told him to expect them shortly. Archie landed right outside the lockup. The sheriff came out to greet them.

"Hey, I know that guy he was a commander of our squad. When deployed," He sent us on a suicide mission we didn't know it was until it was too late our intel was all wrong and he knew it. Leave him with me, and I'll make him talk. I've been hoping to get a chance like this. You cost four of my men to lose their lives. I had never lost anyone till I answered to you,"

The sheriff really wanted to get the colonel in a cell and bounce him around a bit. Jake took the sheriff aside.

"Look don't kill him; he has info we need. We can always kill him later."

"I'm going to call an old contact he might be able to get his hands on some sodium pentothal. That will loosen his tongue," Jake was really hoping his friend would come through for him.

The colonel thought he could activate some old comrades with talk. He started to speak and the sheriff, his deputies, Jake, Sam, and Tech all yelled in unison, "SHUT UP," funny they wanted him to talk. Jake figured if the colonel thinks they're really waiting on a drug to make him talk. They play it easy... at first.

"Hey Sam, you ever hear how Casey and I met," Tech knew. But he played it off like he didn't know.

"He came in when you got your own squad. June was with me in my office, and Casey came in, just as June was leaving.

He smiled at her and looked at me. We went through all the introductions and pleasantries," Then he said, "That was fine looking fox that walked out,"

I looked at him and said, "That's my wife Sargent."

"Oh, gee sorry sir. If she ever comes on to me, I will tell you right away, sir."

Sam just started laughing, "that's an honest man."

"That's when I knew we would become friends. He made second in command. You need a sense of humor otherwise you let the job turn you into that," Jake waved his hand in the direction of the colonel. Jake got a call. He made a friend with an intelligence division ten years ago.

He basically said, "The drug is yours if we get him when you're done... alive we want him alive," Jake had to make a quick run with Archie to get the drug. Tech and the sheriff's deputies waited behind at the sheriff's Office. The sheriff went with Jake and Sam.

They arrived at the coordinates and there was a car, a black car, naturally. Jake pulled up alongside the car. Now Jake

Written By
J.R. Wilson

and Archie are the only ones who knew even with the windows down Archie's force field would stop bullets. Driver's side to driver's side. The sheriff was a little anxious.

The driver of the other car said, "Nice car, here this is for you," He handed a small case with a handle on top to Jake. Then he drove off. Jake opened it and it had a few needles and little bottles of liquid.

"We're good, let's go," Archie went stealth, and they flew off.

"You know you could have got killed pulling up with your window down and so close," the sheriff commented still shaking.

"It was fine, Archie has a force field even with all the windows down nothing is going through, but a very big but, we can shoot out just stick the barrel out the window and we can shoot them they can't shoot us. Show them Archie," on the screen a picture of Archie came up, and a two-inch haze covers the outside of Archie.

"What you're looking at is the force field. It isn't visible to the naked eye but it's there," Jake explained.

"This car is way weird and I'm having trouble getting my head around it," the sheriff responded.

"Yeah, tell me about it," Jake said, "I spent the first week freaking out. He was always showing me something mind blowing. I fully understand," Jake looked at Sam, you seem to be taking things in stride,"

"Hey, when I'm with you nothing shocks me. I got use to the unusual the first year we served together. You're like a magnet for weird stuff," Sam informed him.

"Huh… I thought it was trouble, a magnet for trouble. Oh well, they aren't that far apart," Jake remarked.

"How much can Archie take," asked the sheriff.

Written By
J.R. Wilson

The Adventures of
Jake & Archie

"I don't know, we have never reached that point. But I would say maybe a 20mm what probably kick him around a little. The nanites keep everything fixed as we go it's pretty dang cool." Jake explained.

"Nanites," the sheriff repeated.

"Yep, they make up the whole car, you're sitting on them from the rubber in the tire to the roof it's all nanites,"

"If I'm going into a situation, that I think will injure Archie. I check with them ahead of time. They are the most fearless little guys. They have a sense of humor to," A picture of "thumbs up" came up on the dash screen, "We're back," Jake announced. They landed back at the sheriff's Office. Jake, Sam, and the sheriff got inside. Everyone in one piece.

Mean time the man in the black car that gave them the case was waiting outside the gate with another car. The man inside the black car was talking on his cell. "I have no idea where they went, there's only one way in and one way out. We waited thirty minutes. I'm going back inside," After driving around inside he realized that Jake was gone.

"We're headed in, call it a night they gave us the slip I just don't know how," The two cars drove off.

"Everyone is fine, we didn't even smack the colonel around," Casey responded a little bummed.

"Go get him time for his shot," Jake couldn't wait. Deputies brought in the colonel sat him down hands and feet cuffed they weren't taking any chances. Jake administered the

Written By
J.R. Wilson

truth serum. When Jake brought up leaks in the intelligence community. You couldn't get the colonel to shut up. He spilled his guts, like he was going to win a prize for talking. That's probably because Jake told him he would win a prize for talking. Under the drug the colonel acted like a child. They discover this guy's got issues.

He gave the names of his contacts, and some other officials who were getting cash payments. He went on, and on it was crazy. After the guys were looking at their notes and talking a reality hit them. They didn't know who to give this information to. Who do you trust? Jake called his friend to meet him and give him the live colonel.

Sam loaded up the colonial. They drove to the same spot, where they met the black car. It was waiting, Archie pulls up, and Jake gets out and opens the back door. The colonel is so groggy, when Jake helps him up. Jake had a syringe with quiet a lot of serum. He stuck it in the colonel's butt cheek. The colonel barely felt it. Jake helped him in the car and handed the drugs back to the man. Jake got back in Archie and waited for the black car to leave, but they sat there. Jake just put Archie in gear and drove off. Thinking something is amiss, he tells Archie head out and then drive fast, out of sight of the black car. Outside the gate the other car was back, it was waiting, and the black car came up from behind.

"Well Archie… what you got in your bag of tricks,"

"What's wrong with the EMP. That will stop them," Archie replied.

Jake was good with that, "So let us have it Archie boy," A bit of a boom went off and the cars were stopped, "Good job my friend," Jake was satisfied.

As they passed the other black car, they could see the men were frantically trying to figure out what happened. Once

Written By
J.R. Wilson

around the turn, stealth on and gone, they were headed for the ranch. In the black car the colonel was slobbering and mumbling. The man was trying to call for help, but his cell was cooked. Pretty soon the colonel slumped over in the back seat and was gone. Jake kept his word; he gave the colonel to the man in the black car alive. Wasn't Jakes fault if he didn't stay that way. Besides, he couldn't have that big mouth colonel talking about Archie.

I wonder what they were trying to do, Jake was thinking. I've known this guy for over twenty years something is really messed up. Back at the ranch. Jake and Archie were talking.

"So, Jake have you got an idea what you friend is up to."

"No, I'm going to find out, one way or another," Jake gets on his cell and calls his old friend. Jake wasn't a happy camper, finding out he can't trust anyone. The voice answered.

"What about our agreement Jake, the colonel is dead."

"That's unfortunate, what did you do," Jake asked innocently.

"I didn't do anything when my agents showed up with him, he was dead."

"He was alive when I handed him over to your agent. So… tell me what the idea behind the two black cars was," Jake wasn't going to let this go.

"I don't what you mean bro."

"Don't bro me, those guys wanted to end me," Jake was getting upset, "Fine you want to lie to me, you know how that works… RIGHT," there was a long pause. Jake had to look at his phone to be sure that the line hadn't disconnected. Seeing it was still an active call he put it back up to his face and said, "I'm coming for you."

"Oh, really you don't know where I am. I'm in charge now, so you need to adjust your attitude,"

Written By
J.R. Wilson

The Adventures of
Jake & Archie

Now Jake is hot and angry. He hung up the phone and asked Archie.

"Did you trace him," Jake knew he had. Archie always traces calls.

"We got him, heading to the city Jake," Archie was dialed in on the voice's location. Since Sam and Vicki were staying at the ranch. Jake grabbed Sam.

"You're coming with me brother, we are going for a visit," Sam and Jake jumped into Archie, and they were off.

In a matter of minutes, Archie had them right over the location. They were stealth mode in the middle of the city. Jake spotted his old friend. He was getting in the car right below Archie. There is an open space behind the car. Jake had Archie drop down long enough for Sam to jump out and walk up to the car. He walked up and opened the passenger door.

"Hi, I thought that was you," and climbed in the passenger side. The Jakes friend looked at Sam and was acting like he was glad to see him.

"How you been Sam."

"Fine just fine," then Sam pulled out his .9 mm, pointed it at Jakes old friend and said, "Drive."

"What's up Sam why are you doing this."

Sam was quiet. Then he looked at the driver and told him to head to the parking lot at the fed building, "Go to the top floor and park."

"What's going on Sam," the driver asked.

"Shut up and drive," Sam was all in. When it came to dealing with a treacherous creep, a back stabber. This guy was supposed to be Jakes friend. When they reached the top floor of the parking lot, Jake was waiting. Sitting on Archies hood just standing by. When Sam got out of the car, "He's all yours Jake."

Written By
J.R. Wilson

"I appreciate that Sam," Jake walked over to his old friend and hit him with a right cross that floored him.

"Good to see you," Jake was really feeling good after he punched his old friend.

Laughing, Jake grabbed him and slammed him into his black car, "So aren't you glad to see me? huh! I didn't think so," Jake was trying to keep control. "What are you up to," Jake asked his old friend.

"I just saw an opportunity when you said, you had the colonel I thought I could get in on it."

"That's bull, now start talking. Haven't you wondered why we're on the top floor," Jake wasn't playing he wanted answers, "There are two ways you're getting off this roof. One you drive down. Two you fly down," Jake smiled.

"We have been watching the colonel for a while now. We suspected he was a leak; we just didn't have proof."

"That doesn't explain the two black cars coming after me."

"Those guys were doing that on their own," Jakes friend insisted.

"I don't buy that... do you Sam."

"No Jake, he's hiding something," Sam didn't trust him a bit.

"Fine let's toss him off and I have another stop to make," Jake's friend started talking away and Archie was recording it, "Okay... okay, shut up dang-o," Jake had an idea, "Load him into Archie, we will take him with us," Jake was calling the President.

"Hi Jake, what can I do for ya," The President sounded happy.

"Hi, Mr. President, we need to talk I'm right outside. I've got a scum bag with me, who I thought was my friend. He just

Written By
J.R. Wilson

tried to get me killed," Archie set down on an outside verandah. Jake, Sam, and the trader got out. Jake explained all he knew to The President. He also told him he didn't know who to give the names to, the colonel gave him. He couldn't trust anybody.

The President understood and had the Secret Service come up and take custody of what used to be Jake's friend. The President told Jake they had been watching this guy. He had been running his own operations without clearance. They thought he was committing treason. Jake gave the list the colonel had given under truth serum. The President looked the list over and it was not a surprise.

"We suspected a few of these names. There's a couple on here we didn't know about."

"It's on you now. I wash my hands of all this internal junk. I hope that list helps," Jake and Sam climbed into Archie, and they left.

"That may have done some good and if not, it should have. Anyway, not our problem now," Jake is feeling better. Jake looked at Sam, "Thanks for your help you're still a good man Sam."

Sam said, "Glad to help and I appreciate you letting us stay at the ranch. Can we swing by our house, Vicki needs some of overnight stuff and clothes."

Jake replied, "Not a problem."

Jake and Sam headed for Sam's house. They landed and drove up to his house. When they pulled up onto the driveway Jake saw movement in the house. Sam jumped out gun drawn and approached the back door. Jake went around to the front door. They had keys so no busting down doors. They quietly entered the house. Jake signaled Sam to cover him. Jake went quietly down the hall. When a guy burst out of the master bedroom Jake close-lined him, he went down hard. It was a Ukrainian.

"What the hell are you doing here," Sam hollered at him.

At first, he wouldn't say a thing. Jake offered this, "If he's not talking, let's just shoot him."

"Good idea. To save time we can drop him off with the sheriff after we shoot him," Sam liked this plan one less mafia creep to deal with.

"Wait don't shoot me. I'm the last of the family alive. I can't even get hold of my contacts to get me out of here. I came here because I knew the house was empty and I was hungry. I was going to cook some food. I have nowhere to go. The family hired me a month ago. I have no loyalty to them. I just want to go home."

"Where's home," Jake inquired.

"Ukraine," He answered.

"What's your name," Sam asked.

"Ivan," he answered.

"Ok Ivan, maybe we can use you," Jake continued, "If I give you chance how do I know, I can trust you."

"I never liked those mafia types I just need the money. If I work for you, will you protect me and my family," Ivan was a little nervous. Jake is having trouble with Ivan's accent, but he gets the gist of what he's saying.

"We protect our own, Okay, where's your family," Jake asked.

"They are in Ukraine my family is very poor," Ivan wouldn't stop talking.

"It will be hard to get them out of Ukraine," Ivan continues, "I left them with my Papa in the country."

"Can you call them," Jake asked.

"Yes, oh yes," Ivan was anxious.

Written By
J.R. Wilson

"Okay Archie you're the interpreter. Give Archie the phone number,"

Ivan did just that. Archie put a call through. Their conversation was heartfelt and sincere. After talking to his wife. Ivan said. "She and the kids will be ready. How soon do they leave."

"Tell them to get ready now, we will pick them up in about an hour," Jake informed Ivan.

Ivan just stared at Jake. "That's not possible. It's an all-day flight."

"Just tell her," Jake insisted, "Archie, you got the GPS. Where are they."

Archie answered, "Yes I do, when do we leave."

"As soon as we drop off Sam and Vicki's stuff at the ranch."

So, they helped Sam bring out his things, then they left for the ranch. At the ranch Jake made a discovery. After talking with Ivan. Jake found out Ivan was a very popular chef in his hometown.

"Maybe we should have let him cook at Sam's."

"Alright I need Ivan and Casey. Anyone else want to come," Jake announced. Casey spoke Russian. It wasn't guaranteed that Ivan's family spoke Russian, but it was a fair guess.

"I will," Sam spoke up.

"Fine, say Ivan how many will be coming back," Jake wondered.

"My wife and two sons. Maybe my parents but I doubt they will leave their farm," Ivan replied in a heavy Ukrainian Accent.

Jake was still having some trouble understanding everything Ivan says. "Load up," Jake hollered. Ivan was confused, he didn't know how they would get home so quickly in a car. He thought maybe Jake doesn't know how far away Ukraine is, "Ivan, I need you to understand something, and this goes for your whole family," Jake needed to know if they could keep a secret. Ivan assured him any secret was safe with him and his family. They were raised keeping secrets. Where they live it's a matter of survival. "Good enough let's go," said Jake.

Archie rolled out to the driveway then he went stealth. Jake turned on the green button and Archie shot right up in minutes they were in orbit. Ivan was all bug-eyed and shacking like a leaf. Jake turned to him and said, "Easy boy, its fine your perfectly safe if this. Bothers you wait till we load up to come back," Sam was wondering what that meant.

They started their descent and were about a half mile from Ivans Papa's farm, so they set down and drove like any other car. They arrived at the farm and Ivan couldn't believe it.

"You American's have technology like no other country on Earth. This is amazing," Ivan said.

Jake laughed, "Yeah we Americans are pretty high tech," Everyone came running out. A lot of hugs and kissing.

"This is my wife Kateryna and our sons Bohdan and Danylo. This is Andrly my Papa."

"Pleased to meet you sir," Jake and Sam were being very polite.

"This is my Mama Diana."

"Nice to meet you," she said.

"You taking care of my son," in very heavy accent.

"We are doing our best ma'am."

"Is everyone packed," Ivan asked his boys. Who were very young and didn't want to let go of their Papa.

"We are ready Papa," said the youngsters.

The Adventures of
Jake & Archie

"Load up everyone, are you coming along Andrly? Theres plenty of room for you and Diana."

Andrly looked at the car and said, "No, how will you get everyone and their luggage in that car."

Jake walked to the trunk, "You would be surprised how much trunk space this car has," Andrly was watching as Jake just kept putting more, and more into the trunk. He walked over to take a look. When he saw Casey at the portal door carrying stuff down he almost fainted.

"What is this? How can that be," Andrly asked in total shock.

Ivan spoke up, "These Americans have very advanced technology Papa. But you must keep this secret understand Papa."

"Oh… yes, top secret, we will keep to us," Papa promised. In a heavy accent.

"Everybody on board your sons and wife can ride down in the realm. It will be less upsetting for them on the trip,"

"Sound like fun boys," Ivan asked.

"Oh yes we would like that," The boys were already going down into the portal. Ivan joined them and his wife.

"Ok Sam, Casey let's head for home," Jake declared.

"Andrly if you need us just call, we will come as fast as we can. Believe me, that's dang fast." Jake told them in case bad things happen.

"Here these are Kateryna and the boys' passports. Keep my family safe for me. I will miss them so much."

"Listen if you want to come for a visit just call," Jake offered.

"Andrly and I have no passports so we can't leave," Diana said disappointed.

Written By
J.R. Wilson

The Adventures of
Jake & Archie

"Don't worry, we can get around that, no problem. We don't use a port of entry. We go from here right to my ranch no stops," Jake was trying to explain.

"How is this possible," Diana asked.

"It's our technology it's all very secret," Jake said.

"When you are safe, get Ivan to cook for you. He is best Chef. He will make you Borshch and Salo, Dervny, Holubtsi these are wonderful dishes. You try okay."

Jake was making a little headway. Diana still looked confused.

"Archie goes stealth," Jake instructed, "Now reappear and float up about thirty feet then land," Archie did what he was told. Diana and Andrly were just staring. That's right, the bugged eyes and jaw hanging open. They understood that Jake must be a very special person to have such a car.

Jake smiled and spoke. It's been an honor," They took off and blasted up through the clouds overhead. Then... They were out of sight. Andrly and Diana looked at each other just shook their heads and went in the house.

Archie is reaching the edge of the atmosphere. He begins to level out. Going against the earth's rotation. He starts down. It's much quicker than racing, the rotation:
It's a slow descent Archie doesn't like getting heated up. They go up in five minutes; they come down in about thirty minutes. Somehow that seems wrong. They start their approach to the ranch. Archie set down by the barn. When everyone exited the trunk. They walked around looking.

"Where are we," Kateryna asked very confused.

"You're on our ranch in Colorado best state in America," Jake bragged.

"How did we get here so fast," she was little dizzy.

Written By
J.R. Wilson

152

The Adventures of
Jake & Archie

Ivan was helping inside so she could lie down. When
they entered the barn, they couldn't believe their eyes.

"This is a house where are the animals," Kateryna was
tired and overwhelmed. Ivan laid her down on the couch.

The boys were checking out the games, "Can we play."

"Sure, why not," Jake said. He figured they would play a
video game, but they went for the pool table.

Strange. He thought. They're from Ukraine maybe that's
a Saturday night for them. You can make yourself at home,
there's two rooms that aren't being used on the right and has a
king bed and the other has bunk beds. Over there on the left
there's a kitchen where it should have food, if not just come to
the house. There's a bar if you need a drink. The guys come in
and out of here just a warning. It's sort of their playhouse.

Archie was signaling. Jake was tired and he approached
Archie outside the barn.

"So, what's so important," Jake was wanting to go to
bed. "We got a call from the Amorlites, there seems to be a large
ship headed for their planet. It's a huge destroyer they want and
need our help," Archie reported.

"I need to get some rest," Jake was dead on his feet.

"Okay, we are leave in the morning," Archie announced.
Jake gave him a smile and went inside right to his bedroom.
Jake woke up the next day. He could smell coffee.
There was something else a faint he could barely hear. It
sounded like Archie then it occurred to Jake his ear pod must
have fallen out if his ear. He searched through the bed and
pillows. Then he looked down and there it was under the edge of
the bed; he probably knocked it down there rummaging around
on the bed.

Written By
J.R. Wilson

Chapter 22
Back to the Alien Planet

"We have to get going Jake," He could hear Archie and realizing they should be flying by now," Sorry about that Archie I'll be right out," When Jake got to the barn all the guys were standing around like they were waiting for something.

"I'm headed to the Amorlites planet seems they have an invading space craft coming at them," Jake said in haste.

"We want to come," Casey requested.

"You can't all come, two of you must stay here. I'm not leaving June unprotected,"

After a few, rock, paper, scissors rounds, Casey and Sam won. Jake wanted supplies. He asked Rusty to get the fifty-quart ice box, fill it up with bottled waters, Gatorades, just drinks in general and sleeping bags, camping gear and ammo. Jake grabbed his Henry and the Judge and what he called his hog leg, a .22 magnum six shooter. He liked that gun because he always hit his target. Even on the run. The hollow point is filled with an explosive Casey came up with. Rusty's always trying to improve the explosion but hasn't had much luck. So, it's a .22 magnum with a kick. They loaded up but kept all supplies in the trunk not the portal. Jake wasn't sure what they were getting

Written By
J.R. Wilson

into, he wanted to be ready for anything. Getting to the gear in a hurry. It might be crucial.

"Let's go! We are already late! Maybe too late… we could be heading to a dead planet," Archie took off like he was shot out of a gun. Jake had to reach, and it wasn't easy, for the green button. He finally hit it. and everything was once again relaxed like sitting in your living room at home. No inertia. "Gotta love that button," Jake laughed.

Sam and Casey put all their faith in Jake. He always brings them home. They never need to worry. They looked at Jake and he was sleeping.

In a couple hours Archie woke all three of them. Approaching portal prepare to slip and a door opened, and Archie slipped right in and in a few moments slip right out into the Amorlites galaxy and Right into a huge ship coming out of another portal. It was so big, it got in Archie's way. That thing is at least two city blocks across and twice as long as Jake was thinking. The ship and Archie bumped, and the ship opened fire on Archie, it was hitting him and taking little chunks out of his exterior. Which was strange, Archie was in stealth mode

"Archie hit the sucker with your laser. The big one and hurry." Jake shouted.

Archie fired the ten-inch solid beam. He started slicing up the invading ship like a pizza. Just pieces floating in space.

"Archie is in trouble! He's losing power! Archie is there anywhere near that we can land on and hopefully breath," Jake asked staying calm.

"Yes. But it will take a lot of what power I have left," Archie warned.

"What other options do we have? We must get you on the ground," Jake and the guys looked at each other and nodded in agreement. Achie put the peddle down and they were hitting

close to light speed. Only for a few moments, that's all it took.
When Archie slowed down. The planet was getting closer fast.
The car was doing fine; it began to slow down. Archie brought
them down easily. He hovered and then lowered down till they
touched.

"Go get the gear out of the trunk! Move! I'm not sure
what's going on with Archie. Archie, you with me," Jake was
really concerned.

"Yes Jake. But I think... I this.," Archie was struggling
to get out the words.

As Jake was closing the door he could feel panic welling
inside of him. He asked, "What is it Ar..." and then the door
just turned to dust right in his hand. The rest of the car followed.
Just a pile of dust. Jake stood there, on a strange planet looking
at Sam and Casey. Archie was just... gone. Jake and guys just
looked at each other not knowing what to do.

ARCHIE WAS GONE !!

"What now Jake," Casey asked, "Are we stuck here."

"I think temporarily we are stuck," Jake was trying to
remember. *What was it Archie said about dust?* "Oh wait. I
recall something about lightning," Jake was having a problem
remembering.

"What is that? You hear that Jake," Sam asked.

Casey went over to a small hill and started climbing it.
When he got to the top he yelled back, "We got trouble," Jake
and Sam ran over to Casey.

"What the heck is that?" Sam asked.

"I don't know, but they look hungry," Jake pointed it out.
What they are seeing is a huge amount of what looked like giant
wolves. But these had larger teeth and had matted fur. There
were thousands of them.

The Adventures of
Jake & Archie

"Looks like we found out why there's no civilization…
they were eaten. These things are as big as Saint Bernards,"
Casey said nervously.

"You guys got all the weapons out of Archie right," Jake
asked.

"Yep, even the mini," Casey said.

"You guys get on the hill and make their lives
miserable," Jake instructed, "I have an idea. I remember it takes
a big charge of electricity. This planet is affecting my mind it's
hard to concentrate," Jake paused rubbing his temples. His eyes
snapped open, and you could almost see the light bulb go on,
"Wait! I've got it," he reached into his cargo pants pocket. He
pulled out the taser Archie gave him for protection, "Archie told
me this puts out over a hundred and fifty thousand volts. Let's
see… how do you turn on this thing," Jake could hear the mini
going off and Sam was firing the grenade launcher. Jake turned
on the taser and walked over to the pile of dust. "This has to
work," Jake mumbled to himself.

He held the taser like a staff. With the electrical side
down, he slammed it into the dust that remained of Archie. He
could feel the crackle around his feet, but he held it to the dirt.
This was their only hope of returning home within Jake's
lifetime.

Then a loud snap and poof the car was back.

"What the? How did you do that Jake," Sam was blown
away by what he saw.

"I don't know. I just remembered that Archie said
something about electricity would restore him if it was done in
less than an hour after he was turned to dust," said Jake. He was
a little blown away by this also. He hadn't expected this to work
so quickly.

Written By
J.R. Wilson

"You think that's why he gave me the taser," asked Casey.

"Archie, can you hear me," Jake yelled.

"Yes, no need to yell," Archie replied.

"You guys doing okay up there," Jake hollered.

"Yeah, getting low on ammo though," Casey kept firing.

"Archie what are all those streaks going through you. Red, green, blue and yellow," Jake thought he was watching a light show.

"Those are nanites racing around trying to find where they belong," Archie informed Jake.

"How long is that going to take? We need to get the hell out of here,"

"I don't know," Archie stated.

"You don't know... Archie that's not an answer," Jake knew Archie wasn't himself, "Archie can you still phase,"

"I believe so," Archie said. Jake could hear the confusion in Archie's response. The irony of a confused electronic item was not lost on Jake. *I have a concussed car* Jake thought to himself. He couldn't help but smile. He chuffed out a small laugh before composing himself.

"Well maybe if you phase the nanites would find it easier to get to their assigned spots," he offered this with a question in his voice, but Archie took it as an absolute.

"Thats a good idea Jake, why didn't I think of that," Archie wondered. Archie started to phase out and after a few seconds he phased back in. "Wow Jake... your idea worked," Archie was back to his old self physically.

"Come on guys. Load up, grab what you can and get in," Jake hollered. When Archie lifted off, he swung around to see the attacking animals.

Written By
J.R. Wilson

The Adventures of
Jake & Archie

"Archie unload on those things, let's thin them out," said Jake.

"Ok Jake," Archie was firing everything he had.

"Ok wait. What are they doing they stopped attacking," Jake was looking out the windshield watching the animals consume their own. "It looks like their eating their dead..." he trailed off as he took on the spectacle. Jake found it interesting that their numbers were so high given their propensity for cannibalism. "I'm not sure how I feel about this? We killed them, but it was in self-defense," Jake continues, "So we aren't murderers and apparently, we fed them. So maybe they get a taste for each other and like it. They can kill each other for food."

Jake and the guys started to laugh. Archie was back on course for the Amorlites planet. Jake knows something isn't right with Archie, it's no wonder all this car has been through. Maybe the scientists that created him can give him a look. As they approached the Amorlites planet they were receiving a transmission from, the Amorlites. Archie put it on speaker. Jake wanted everyone to hear.

"Welcome back we are happy you came to help. We have been monitoring the battle, then we lost you. We thought you were destroyed. We are very happy you are not. We will be waiting for your final approach," The Amorlites communication didn't sound right. Jake, Casey and Sam noticed it right away. Notably Archie carried on without making observations about how unusual the message seemed.

"Men I'm not sure what to expect. Friend or foe," Jake laughed, "Don't worry we can handle this," As they started down into the atmosphere two ships came out to greet the trio. Jake remarked, "Safeties off this is unusual."

Written By
J.R. Wilson

The Adventures of
Jake & Archie

The ships were communicating with Archie, and it seemed everything is fine. As they got closer there was a huge crowd of Amorlites, they were everywhere. They set down in the same spot they landed on their last visit. When Jake rose out of Archie the crowd went wild. They were so glad to see Jake again. Cheers and streamers, it looked like downtown New York after World War two. It was a sight to remember. Then Jake saw someone he knew, the scientists.

"Hello Jake," the lead scientist seemed glad to see him, maybe everything is fine after all.

Jake asked him, speaking very loudly, "Can we go somewhere and talk?"

"Yes, come with me," the scientist yelled back.

The three guys followed him into a very unusual building. It was like a bunch of triangles put together with seven points of the building going towards the sky.

"Nice to see you again," Jake started.

"Yes its, good to see you Jake," the scientist replied.

"I need a little favor," Jake asked.

"Sure, anything, we owe you so much, but first who is this with you," the scientist queried.

"Oh sorry, this is Sam he is a very good friend," Jake said, "You remember Casey."

"Oh yes, how are you Casey," asked the scientist.

"Always good," Casey smiled.

"What do you need Jake," the scientist was very willing to help.

"I need you to check on Archie. He's been through a lot," said Jake. He was hoping they could help.

"Sure, let's get him over to our lab," The scientist directed.

Written By
J.R. Wilson

The Adventures of
Jake & Archie

Jake and the rest got into Archie and drove over to the lab it wasn't far, a few blocks.

Once they pulled inside, the other scientists were working on something. Jake didn't have a clue. They gathered around Archie with what appeared to be test equipment of some kind. The scientists started looking at each other with concern. Jake figured out their facial expressions from being around them so much.

"What's wrong," Jake asked.

"It is looking like his power cell was damaged. What happened out there," the scientist wanted to know.

Jake explained the battle and the planet and using the taser to bring Archie back and the phasing to get the nanites in line.

"Wow how did you know to do all that?" the scientist was extremely impressed.

"I don't know… some of the things Archie told me, and I guess some dumb luck helped," Jake replied.

"The good news is we have another power pack on hand, so we jack him up and plug in a cord to keep him powered up while we change the pack," replied the scientist. Archie raised up on what looked like a very skinny jack. The scientist plugged in a clear cord with something flowing through it. Something green and blue. Jake watched closely. One of the scientists walked over and opened a big drawer. Inside was a complete power pack ready to install. As the scientists removed the old power pack from under Archie. These packs are about eight inches thick and three feet by five feet.

"You guys just happen to have a spare power cell? For a prototype car," Jake askes. There is some suspicion tickling the back of his mind, "You guys building another car."

Written By
J.R. Wilson

The Adventures of
Jake & Archie

The scientist kept working and finally one of them came over to Jake, "Yes, we are building another car. It won't be like Archie. Not as many options, isn't that what you call them,"

"We want it for interstellar travel," another scientist contributed.

"Fine, so all you did was replace his power cell and that's it. No new surprises," Jake asked skeptical.

"No updates. No applications. Nothing new Jake," the scientist reassured him.

"Are we good to go," Sam asked.

"I believe we are," Jake said while getting into Archie.

"Archie how are you feeling?" Casey asks.

"Like brand new. I haven't felt like this since the day I was put together," Archie was feeling it he wanted to fly.

"Alright Archie let's go home," Jake couldn't believe what they went through on this trip.

"Archie did you scan that planet we almost got stuck on," Casey was curious.

"Somewhat… not a thorough scan. I wasn't at peak performance at the time," Archie replied, "Why?"

"I was just wondering if the population of those meat-eating monsters had changed," Casey asked idly. He was more curious than he was putting on, but it was more to see what impact they had on the ecosystem.

"Should we swing by just close enough for a scan," Jake was also curious, but more about why Casey was. Archie was right on top of it. They altered course just enough for Archie's scanners to work.

"Huh," Archie was sounding more like himself. The chipper sound of his enthusiastic self-echoed through the cabin.

"Huh? What's with the Huh? Archie," asked Jake.

Written By
J.R. Wilson

The Adventures of
Jake & Archie

"I'm not reading any life down there. That's what the huh was for," Archie sounded grumpy. Jake knew Archie was back to his old self.

"Should we take a closer look," Jake was giving everyone a vote.

"Sure, why not. I'm getting curious myself," Sam spoke up.

Casey said, "I'm in let's check it out."

"Move in closer Archie. Let's get a closer look," Jake said. As Archie came closer to the planet, pings from the life form detection started to sound off.

"Archie what form of life are you seeing. Is it those monster wolf looking creatures," Jake asked.

"No this is different. These readings are new; I wasn't getting these, last time we were here. I'm reading something close to human," Archie said with some surprise in his voice.

"Shall we venture down and check it out," Jake suggested.

"Why not one more thing to deal with… as if we didn't have enough," said Sam.

Archie landed near the readings.

"You guys see anything," Casey was looking all around.

"No, it looks safe to get out," Jake said hoping he's right.

"Hello," a strange voice called, "you came back."

"Yes, we came back we were worried we might have messed up your evolution or something," Jake answered. From around a huge boulder came a little alien, about five foot tall he seemed glad to see the guys. He seemed to be having trouble seeing.

"Are you alright," asked Sam.

"Oh yes, my eyes are taking a while to adjust. We haven't been out of the caves in a long time. Thanks to you guys we are free from those beasts, and we can come out," The little guy was so grateful. He is covered in dark clothing and has a kind of a hat on his head. They were like the Amorlites. Maybe they are a distant relation.

"What do we call you," Jake asked.

"We are the Coot. We lived in caves because of the beasts. My name is Roshee. Thank you again for taking care of the beasts."

"Are you folks ok? Do you need anything," Jake asked.

"No, we are fine now. Thanks to you. It will take time to adjust. But we have all we need. We just need to start work on the surface," Roshee explained.

"We were just here not too long ago, how did those beasts become extinct so fast," Casey asked.

"They ate each other, it was amazing to watch. They just went for one to the other killing each other. It finally came down to a couple big ones, left and they tore each other apart. It all happened so fast," Roshee went on to explain, "Do you want to see our caves? We have tunnels leading all over our planet some are over two hundred miles long."

"How do we understand each other's language," Casey asked.

"We have built in interpreters. They can interpret any language. There are five different languages on our planet, so you see we always have our interpreters on."

"Well, we have to get home," Jake told the Coot, "But we will be back at some point, when we have more time."

Chapter 23
A Home Coming

  While Archie was ready to go the guys were given some
gifts from the Coot.
  "This is very nice of you to give us these things. Thank
you so much. We have nothing to give you in return. When we
come back, we will bring you some things from our planet,"
Jake promised.
  "That is not necessary. You saved our planet we will
never forget you," Roshee was very grateful.
  "Bye for now. We will be back," Jake and the guys said
their farewell. Archie took off and was bound homeward.
  "Am I wrong, or did we save two planets on this
adventure," Casey remarked.
  "We defiantly saved two planets on this trip," Archie
confirmed.
  They approached the location where Archie can finally
launch the portal. Archie did his navigator thing, and they
slipped through and then out of the other side of the portal back
in their own galaxy.

Written By
J.R. Wilson   165

The Adventures of
Jake & Archie

"Ok we have a two-and-a-half-hour ride home. Do you have any more hunting story's from when you were a boy Jake," Casey asked he thought it would kill some time.

"I could tell you about the first bird my springer puppy retrieved," Jake suggested, "My brother Victor and I were hunting pheasants. We had just come in from a hunt with some city dudes that always come out for opening weekend. They wanted to rest for the late afternoon hunt; old guys need their nap. Most of them hadn't hit a thing. Victor and I had each got four birds and we weren't tired. We draw out the birds and hang them to drain.

We headed out behind the ranch house and worked the ditches surrounding the harvested rice field. Victor's dog was the mama to my pup. So, he didn't wander away, he was only six months old. He wasn't much of a hunter or retriever yet. So, we worked the first ditch full of tools, Vic's dog was working the ditch and flushed out a couple birds, and we dropped them. His dog retrieved the birds. I moved forward and stepped right on a tail feather and the bird flew straight up and I pulled to shoot but I hadn't reloaded. I quickly slammed a shell in my twelve gauge and hit the button to close the chamber. I aimed and shot. The bird came down.

Now my puppy was out in the field to my left just playing and frolicking around, when the bird I shot came right down and landed on my dog. He jumped and yiped and stood back barking at the bird. Vic and I were laughing. My puppy kept looking at me then the bird. He couldn't pick it up, but not for the lack of trying. So, he got his mouth around the pheasant near its head and picked it up. He half picked it up, and half dragged it to me. When he got to me, he spit it out and just started barking away, looking at me then the bird. This was so funny because I knew exactly what he was saying with all his

Written By
J.R. Wilson

166

barking. He was saying, 'I was in the field minding my own business when for no apparent reason this feathery thing hit me from above. I wasn't even looking! I thought I should bring it over and show it to you.' Victor and I were laughing so hard and my puppy looked at me like I was nuts.

My dad wasn't big on having critters mounted or stuffed, but this bird was that exception," Jake paused for a moment.

"That's a good story, is it true," Casey asked.

"Of course it's true. Look... every time I tell you guys a story. You ask if it's true. First off, I've never lied to guys about anything. Second, any story I tell you from my youth is true. Maybe I misremember some stuff but it's not intentional. But when I tell a story its dead on, the way I remember it."

"There's more to the story its funny too. One of the city hunters had missed every shot he fired. I told him no Biggy we got a dozen birds drawn out and hanging. You're welcome to as many as you want. He said, "No! I must shoot it, my wife will know I'm lying, if I tell her I Shot them. She can read me like a book.' I had a plan. We have a friend that raises pheasants. Dad and I drove over to see him and bought five birds from him. We brought them back to the ranch. I said to that city hunter I will release them one at a time, and he will be the only one shooting. I set the bag down and walked over to get a drink out of the garage fridge. When I heard two shots.

I walked out and everyone was laughing. The city hunter just... shot the sack. He got all of them in the two shots he fired. He said, 'Throw them in back, I shot 'em. That's all that matters.' You see what happened there? He was worried and scared of his wife catching him lying. When he shot the birds, he changed, he knew he was good to go, he had confidence in what he was going to tell her. Because of this he went through a sort of metamorphosis. Dad explained it to me that way. And yes, it's a true story," Jake thought he would get out front of the follow up from the boys.

"Ok, okay don't be so sensitive. I was just messing with you," Casey was not questioning Jake. He just liked to piss off Jake from time to time.

"Looks like we're just about home," Archie announced. As Archie got close to the ranch. All Jake could think about was getting a well-deserved rest. When they arrived, everyone was so happy. June handed Jake a hot rum Toddy.

"Everything okay Jake," June asked.

"Yes, everything is… What's the term I'm looking for? Oh yeah. Everything's JAKE," Jake said this loudly with pride. He spread his arms away from himself in the classic look at me stance.

"Ha… very funny. Just as funny as it was in High School," June gave Jake a poke in the side as she spoke, "The boys are in the barn playing pool,"

"Okay that's nice," Jake replied when he looked at June. She was giving him a look that after thirty years and two children Jake had come to know well.

"Oh… okay," he said giving her a knowing smile. Jake got up and headed for bed, June was right behind him.

Chapter 24
The President's Helper

A few weeks later Jake and Archie are in D. C. they
helped find a terrorist. Jake was wondering why they hadn't left.
Waiting on The President he asked Jake to hang around he
wanted to talk to him, about what! Jake had no idea. Then
Archie starts receiving a transmission from Air Force One and
its leaving D.C.

"What the hell," Jake was calling the President.

"Jake, I have a problem can you track us. I may not be
able to communicate with you," then the President was cut off.

"Archie let's get up there. The President needs us," Jake
ordered. Archie was up in no time he maneuvered behind and
above Air Force One. Archie was scanning everything including
listening to conversations on the big jet. Nothing seemed out of
order. Jake is talking to Archie about what to do, "So we wait
and watch just stay with them in case something happens. Keep
your radar reaching out, we need early warning if something is
launched at the President it's up to us. We need to be ready to
take, whatever it is, down!"

"Copy that," Archie responded.

Written By
J.R. Wilson   169

The Adventures of
Jake & Archie

Jake had just finished that sentence when he got his answer.

Archie announced, "Alert incoming, Alert incoming!"

"Okay alert already. Where is it and head for it laser cannons ready," Jake snapped.

"Got it, should I fire," Archie asked.

Jake just stared at the dash in disbelief, "YES! FIRE ALREADY!"

Archie blew the missile out of the sky. The President was calling, "Yes sir." Jake answered, "We just knocked down a missile. We will stay with you as long as it takes."

"Thanks Jake. Your country thanks you and so do I," The President new he was lucky Jake tagged along. Jake still doesn't know what's going on. He feels very uninformed.

Archie called out to Jake, "More missiles… looks like three!"

"Lock on to all three and blast 'em," Jake commanded.

Archie took out the missiles. There was four… one of them got by Archie which is weird. Archie swung around and blasted the rouge missile. It blew up very close to Air Force One. Some fragments hit the outside port engine.

Archie reports to Jake, "We have more company."

"How many," Jake asked.

"Looks like about seventy… maybe eighty. Coming toward the rear of the Jet."

"What are you kidding me that can't be right," this baffled Jake.

"They're little drones each one is an explosive, I can get a lot, but I don't know about all of them?"

Jake says, "Connect me to the pilot."

Archie responds, "You're on boss."

Written By
J.R. Wilson

170

The Adventures of
Jake & Archie

"This is Jake you have a lot… I mean a lot of small drones coming up you're six. I can get some do you have chaff?"

"Yes, we do," The pilot responded.

"On my signal fire the chaff," Jake was waiting for the drones to get close enough where they can't avoid hitting the chaff that's shooting out the back of Air Force One.

"Ok ready… fire," Jake instructed. The chaff comes out so fast it looks an automatic weapon that shooting flares at super speed. Jake was right they got half or more, "Hit it again," Jake commanded.

More chaff flew out, and it took out almost all the rest. Timing was perfect. Jake and Archie were able to mop up any drones that got through. There were only five drones Archie had no problem getting them, Jake, and Archie like dog fights. But first he has Archie fly to where the missiles were coming from. When they arrived above the launcher location. There were two missiles left on the launcher. They weren't regular missiles, these were specials. Theres no time to spare. Archie locked on and transported them to limbo or stasis, anyway, they're not a threat. Jake and Archie could see Air Force One was in trouble. Outside engine on the port side of the plane was smoking.

"Listen we are going to help you with the approach," Jake communicated to the pilot. Jake maneuvered Archie under the left wing near the dead engine. They raised up till they supported the wing.

Co-pilot asks the pilot, "Can you see anything sir?"

"No not a thing but someone is helping. I learned don't question just go with it," the pilot said. Jake figured…
Superman did this same thing. If he could do it so can Archie. Air Force One landed and Archie did what he could and pulled out from under the wing.

Written By
J.R. Wilson

The Adventures of
Jake & Archie

"Archie, you did an outstanding job," Jake was so proud of Archie.

"Let's set down in the parking lot. I need to find out what that was about," Jake declared.

Jake was walking to the terminal after Archie landed. There are a lot of reporters and a big crowd. Jake worked his way through. When he got near a secret service agent. The agent recognized Jake and Actually smiled at Jake.

"I need to talk to the President," Jake said.

"Okay come with me and by the way that was great BBQ you brought us," the agent was willing to help Jake. He knew the President would welcome him.

"Hello Jake," the President was happy to see Jake, "Thank you so much for all you did. You and Archie are a God send."

"That's great! But what the hell was that all about," Jake wanted some answers.

"Come with me," The President requested. They made their way to a private room. The airport provides when the President is in the town, "Jake we have some threats from terrorist. We don't know who yet. Obviously, they are very real. If you and Archie hadn't been there, I wouldn't be here," the President was a bit nervous. He was trying to hide it, but Jake could tell.

"What do you know about this group or individual," Jake was wanting to find these guys.

"Not much we know it's a group that arrived in our country… Somehow," the President said, "I'm meeting with Homeland Security, but everyone is in the dark."

"I'm going to look into this Mr. President," Jake said trying to reassure the President everything will be fine.

Written By
J.R. Wilson

The Adventures of
Jake & Archie

"Jake, I have something for you," The President handed Jake a small fancy box. Jake opened it, there is a U. S. Marshalls badge inside.

"Wow… what's the deal with this," Jake was overwhelmed.

"That's for you. Maybe it will make things easier for you to investigate. You need some authority when you're looking into things for me," The President was happy to give the badge to Jake, he also gave him three deputy badges. Jake wouldn't take money. This is the only thing the President could come up with to reward Jake. Casey, Tech, and Rusty will like this. Plus, Jake made sure his guys get paid and get Benefits. Jake headed back to the parking lot. Archie had been monitoring radio signals, cellphones and any conversations in the parking lot.

"Let's go Archie. Oh… wait look what the President gave me," Jake showed Archie the badge.

"What… you're a U.S. Marshall now," Archie was curious about this, "Does that mean we answer to the President and the Marshalls?"

"We will always answer to the President. He's the President! But we are independent, this badge is to help us when we deal with law enforcement," Jake replied.

"We may have a lead Jake," Archie said.

"See that white suburban over there," Archie asked.

"Yeah, what about it," Jake was giving the suburban a hard look.

"I have some recorded conversation from the SUV," Archie commented.

"That's great, get us to the top of the terminal. Let's go stealth and sit and watch, you can keep monitoring," Jake wasn't sure, but being at the airport where the President is visiting after a missile attack! Yeah! The hairs on the back of his neck are at

Written By
J.R. Wilson

attention. Jake kept thinking he might miss dinner. Better call home. Archie had June on the line.

"Hey babe! Looks like I'm going to be late," June didn't say anything.

Then in a quiet whisper she said, "It's okay, I'll keep something warm for you. Are you in any trouble?"

"Thanks babe, no nothing I can't handle. It's a lot of hurry up and wait like being back in the service," Jake chuckled.

"Gotta go, see you in a little bit. Love you," June said.

"Jake! Those guys are getting out of the white SUV. They have high explosives in those backpacks," Archie was ready to fire.

Jake said, "No wait! I'm guessing that would set off an explosion, a very big explosion. Can you beam those two up and hold them in limbo, or whatever you call it?"

"Sure Jake."

"Then do it," Jake snapped. Archie beamed them up just as they started toward the terminal, "Alright let's head out to sea and beam them down. They look like they could use a swim," Jake was smiling he might make dinner after all. Archie headed out for about five hundred miles. They made sure nobody was around, including ships for hundreds of miles. "When beaming them down make sure we are out of range, who knows what will happen when you release them from the beam. They might just go BOOM," Jake said this dramatically with a flourish of his hands.

"Good advice there Jake," Archie was trying to be more country.

"They're just floating in the ocean," Jake observed "That's just boring. Where's the BOOM."

"Oh Well," then without warning BOOM and I MEAN BOOM, "Now that's more like it," Jake smiled.

Written By
J.R. Wilson

The Adventures of
Jake & Archie

Jake called. The President and gave him the low down. Stopping a bomber at the airport and getting rid of the bomb. A good day's work.

"Archie take us home it's dinner time," Jake is glad. The President is glad. The airport is safe. Most importantly Jake will make it home for dinner. When Jake and Archie got home. Archie went to the barn; Jake went in the house. He was greeted by June with a kiss. June was going back to the kitchen Jake grabbed her and gently pulled her back and said.

"Why did you whisper on the phone to me."

June answered, "I don't want everyone hearing our conversation its private."

Jake smiled and said, "Good girl. Your always on top of things."

Jake went into the kitchen with June. Ivan and Kateryna were there cooking.

"Wow smells good in here," Jake commented.

"Dinner is almost ready," Ivan declared.

"Great! I'm starving," Jake was ready for some dinner. June and Jake set the table and Ivan started bringing in food. They all sat down. And the food must have been good. There was almost no conversation just a lot of chewing. After dinner everyone went out on the porch.

Jake said, "We landed on a planet. Where all the population lived underground. They said they had tunnels over two hundred miles long. Kinda weird way to live."

Sam threw in his two bits, "Yeah there was these huge beasts. They looked like zombie wolves, very big. We thinned them out some when Jake was bringing Archie back."

June said, "What? Zombie wolves why didn't you tell me Jake," She gave him a smack in the middle of his chest with her hand.

Written By
J.R. Wilson

Jake looked over at Sam, "Big mouth… always saying too much."

"It wasn't how it sounds; We had things under control no risk factors at all," Then he stared at Sam.

Sam got the message. Don't spill the beans if it sounds dangerous.

"So… big news," Jake trying to change the subject. He pulled out his U.S. Marshalls badge and four more deputy badges, the guys didn't know about, "The President made me a U.S. Marshall, and the guys are now officially deputy U.S. Marshalls. Now we are freelance we report to the President. I will tell you what he told me," Jake cleared his throat and straightened up before giving his best impression of the President, "You don't worry about most wanted, unless we call on you for help. You worry about the weirdest. There seems to be enough of that to keep you busy. These badges are to help you when dealing with local law or FBI. They will share information a lot quicker," he paused before resuming his relaxed posture and returning to his own voice, "Guys you'll draw pay and benefits. The President figured it was the least the government could do."

Casey, Tech, and Rusty Wanted to celebrate. They decided to go to town and hit the club. Sam and Vicki went to their room. Sam was exhausted and needed some sleep. Vicki is a pretty woman dark hair and dark complexion. She is half Native American and half Spanish. A wonderful disposition and always wanting to help. About five foot eight and full figured. She worships Sam.

"Hey Jake! We are officially the President's helper," Rusty laughed on their way out the door.

Ivan, the illegal immigrant began to busy himself. Clearly, he was unsure of the status of his family, "Now you are

Written By
J.R. Wilson

law, are we safe to stay? Are you going to send us back? What's going to happen to my family," Ivan couldn't keep himself composed. He was ringing the towel he had been using to clear the table. His hands shook slightly.

"Take it easy Ivan, your good. You aren't going back unless you want to. No one is going to bother you," Jake said. He was trying to assuage the concerns of this poor man. If they returned him now, he would be persecuted by the people who had asked him to take Jake and his family out.

June walked up to Ivan and put a hand on his shoulder. It was for reassurance, but Ivan was still looking at Jake. Kateryna came over to June, and the two women clasped hands briefly, "Jake is going to make sure, now that he's the law, that nothing bad happens. You guys have a home here. For as long as you want," June explained, "Tomorrow will we go to the store. You can stock up the fridge in the barn, with what you like to eat," June continued.

Ivan was coming around he wasn't as scared of being forced to leave anymore. Once June started talking about food. Ivan began to relax. Every week they have been here, June takes them shopping.

Back on the porch it was just Jake and June. The guys went to town. Ivan and Kateryna went to the barn to make sure their boys were in bed.

"Remember the last time it was just us on the porch," June asked.

Jake looked at her and smiled, "You know Sam said, I am a weird magnet I always thought I was a magnet for trouble. I guess a little of both is probably true," they both laughed.

Written By
J.R. Wilson

Chapter 25
We Are Under The Gun

Later that week Archie got a call. It was the Amorlites.
The scientist wanted to meet with Jake. Apparently, they had a
visit from the Coot. Jake and Sam were amazed. When they left
the Coot, they were living in caves, now they were traveling
through space.

"How can that be? It's only been a few weeks," Sam was
in disbelief.

Archie responded, "Yes but time is different there. A day
for us might equal a year for the Coot. Remember our second
visit and all the beasts were gone and the Coot were starting to
live and build on the surface. That was about two days for us but
a lot more time had passed on the Coot planet."

"That means a few weeks for us and that could be years
for the Coot," said Jake.

"What should we do Jake," Sam asked.

"I don't know but in a couple of our years the Coot might
want to invade us. What did the Amorlites want when they
called," Jake asked Archie, "They were in a state of panic, or it
seemed that way."

Written By
J.R. Wilson

The Adventures of
Jake & Archie

"We need to take a trip and check out the Coot planet then go for a visit with the Amorlites," Jake reluctantly reported.

"When do we leave?"asked Sam.

"In the morning, we will need as much rest as we can get," Jake explained.

"What do you think we will find?" Casey asked.

"I don't know, I hope they haven't become a conquering race," Jake was concerned that he may have put the Coot on that road.

That morning everyone was saying goodbyes. Jake was distracted. They loaded up and Archie came back out of the barn. Archie went stealth as the car was taking off.

"Jake what's on your mind you seem a little distracted?" Sam asked.

"It's nothing. Well… it's something my dad told me a long time ago. For some reason it keeps popping into my head," Jake replied.

"What did he say," Casey replied.

"He said this to me," Jake went on, "Son you will meet a thousand or more people in your lifetime, but you will only meet two hundred personalities. I have no idea why I remembered that and it's not the first time. What's it mean?" Jake felt better after he said it out loud.

"I have no response to that," Sam said.

"Maybe meeting aliens wasn't part of that equation… or maybe they are," Casey said.

"It's probably the fact that those aliens keep pulling the wool over my eyes. I couldn't pick up on their deception," Jake is starting to get angry and that's never good… for the other guy, "If we are responsible for the Coot we need to fix it somehow," Jake said with determination. Everyone agreed.

Written By
J.R. Wilson

The Adventures of
Jake & Archie

They finally reached the location for the Portal. Archie did his navigation, and they slipped through in just a few seconds. On the other side Archie picked up another portal, it was the same one belonging to the ship they bumped into on their last trip.

"Archie are they here," Jake asked.

"I believe they are boss," Archie was trying to be serious.

"Hmmm... Do we still have the two missiles in your limbo? I think I found a good place to get rid of them. By the way we need a better name then limbo," Jake was taking great pleasure in the idea of it, "Archie beams those two missiles into that portal. Then set them off. Moving out of here fast I'm pretty sure their nukes, I just don't know how big."

"Why set them off now," Sam wondered.

"Because they can post a new portal but the whole area will be irradiated. It will cause big problems when they try and go through," said Jake.

"How did you know that?" Archie asked.

"Hey, you're not talking to a dummy," Everyone started laughing. That's what they do. Keep it light.

Archie beamed the missiles into the portal then he set them off and Archie throttled up to high speed, and they were gone. All of them could look back and see the explosion as the portal collapsed in on itself. They set their direction for The Coot planet. In no big rush Archie and Jake were thinking.

Jack broke the silence, "Did I tell you the insurance adjuster came by last week. I took him to the colored spot and showed him before and after pictures where the truck was parked and the pile of colored dust. He poked around looking at the ground. Then he looked right at me with a straight face, and said 'You have Alien problems?' I was stunned I stared at my

Written By
J.R. Wilson

180

feet trying to come up with a good answer. A million things were running through my head. I looked up and said just said, 'Well… yeah. How'd ya know,' the guy didn't answer, just pulled out his iPad and approved my claim. They must have had alien problems too," Jake laughing, "Sometimes feels like I'm running behind the rest of the world," he shook his head as he chuckled, "That's fine I like to look before I leap."

Casey says, "Yeah but you always leap."

"I know, I just like to look first," Jake was trying to keep things easy.

The Coot planet was coming up fast. Archie started scanning the planet as soon as they were close enough to get readings. The closer they got, the more detailed his readings became.

"Nothing new to report they have dirt roads and no huge complex above or below ground. There's no way, they have the ability to space travel… yet," Archie reported.

"This good news why don't we head to the Amorlite's planet. We need to get to the bottom of all this," Jake directed. Between the Coot planet and the Amorlite planet Archie picked up a signal.

"Looks like they have visitors. Two no… three ships in orbit," Archie continued his scan.

"How invisible are we? Can we get more invisible Archie," Jake was wondering. He wanted all the advantages he could get.

Archie proposed this, "The system they use for radar, with the tiny molecules that are transmitting. They are all around their ships, we go through even stealth mode they see us pushing through the molecules. We kill the molecules, and it should be clear sailing."

The Adventures of
Jake & Archie

"Good plan there Archie boy," Jake was glad because he didn't plan for three giant ships.

"I can set the EMP on the frequency their using. If I can just find… Oh! There it is. I've found it. I can deploy the EMP," Archie said. Some pride in his voice at his abilities. Jake thought it was funny that a machine, either living or dead, could feel pride.

"Go for it," Jake said.

Archie switched on the EMP, and everything looked like fireflies Archie said it was the molecules burning up. Twinkling lights everywhere. Archie flew through the twinkling spots of light. Lasers firing slicing and dicing the large ships. He was taking out two at the same time then dropped down and hit third from below. He sliced it up and down and side to side he even cut a circle in the third ship. All that was left was a bunch sparking pieces, and some were glowing red hot from the temperature of the laser. Archie turned to go to the surface.

"You hover around Archie and see if we can't pick off some of those ugly creatures," Jake ordered.

"There we go. Looks like about twenty of them gathered. They must be having a meeting. Let's upset their little meeting. Archie let 'em have it," Jake instructed.

Archie flew around blasting one after another. He set his laser for multiple shots he hit ten at one time. When all the aliens outside were gone, Archie landed, and the guys got out and geared up. Archie took off hovering and spotting the aliens. He can identify them by their bone structure. Plus, they were about two feet taller than the Amorlites. It was easy for Archie to locate aliens in structures.

"We got two in the building in front of you," Archie pointed out.

"We got this," Sam said.

Written By
J.R. Wilson

The Adventures of
Jake & Archie

The three of them went inside and snuck up and blasted the two aliens.

"Next," Jake said.

"Building to your north, there are about ten inside. I will stay in position in case they try and run," Archie said standing by. The guy's ease in and start trying to locate the creatures.

"Casey, I have them, join me and Sam," Jake said. He started firing with Sam, they got about six of them. Archie got the other four when they ran, heading out the door Archie took them out.

"Ok guys I'm setting down by the door," Archie informed the guys.

Once in the car Jake said, "Let's go hunting."

They flew around. Archie was scanning everything. Finding two more of those aliens. Archie shot them. After a few minutes there's no sign of any creatures. Well… any living creatures just to be clear.

"Archie take us over by the lab and set down," Jake said.

Landing close to the lab. Jake got out and walked towards the door. The scientists inside were glad to see him.

"How y'all doing," Jake greeted them with a smile.

"We do fine, how is Archie," the scientist asked.

"He's great. Yep, just awesome," Jake was working up to asking about their distress signal saying the Coots were attacking, "Oh hell," Jake worked up to it, "Why did you say the Coots were attacking."

The scientist said, "It was a mistake we thought it was the Coot. When the creatures came down to our planet. We saw we made a bad call."

"Listen we set off two nukes in their portal, it should irradiate their side of the portal for a long time," Jake was letting them know they shouldn't have any more trouble from those aliens.

"Can you handle this from here," Jake asked the scientist.

"Yes, thank you so much for all you've done," said the scientist.

Jake and the guys loaded up in Archie and were going home.

"It will be good to get home," Sam said.

"Man your right about that. This space stuff is getting to me," Casey can feel the total vastness of space. The never ending black with potentially infinite darkness for thousands of light years of travel. Earth was much easier to take in.

The Adventures of
Jake & Archie

Chapter 26
A Funny Thing Happened on the Way Home

During the trip through the Amorlites galaxy. A strange thing happened. Archie lost power and the car was just drifting.

"Archie what happened," Jake asked. He was fidgeting with the dark dash and feeling a slight panic rise in his chest. There was no answer from Archie. They only had the air that was in the cars cab. Jake actually wasn't sure where the air was coming from, when they traveled. He imagined there was some sort of life support system that was always active. The men all shared a similar look. It was something close to a goodbye, but not exactly that. Some doubt rested between them all. It couldn't possibly be the end of the story.

Without warning a huge face, looks like an old man. The face was taking up about five hundred yards of space ahead of them, "Hello Jake. Don't worry, you will be fine, we are maintaining the life support in your car," said the face. It wasn't someone that Jake recognized. He wasn't even sure that it was human.

"Can you hear me," Jake asked.

"Yes, we hear you," the face answered.

"Why do you keep saying 'we' there's just you in front of us," Jake was trying to figure out what the hell is going on.

"We are one entity. We are here and we are everywhere, and yet… we are nowhere," the face said this as if it wasn't just a disembodied head before them.

"Fine, what do want why are we stopped," Jake asked. He was getting annoyed.

Written By
J.R. Wilson

The Adventures of
Jake & Archie

"We wanted to meet you. You have managed to save your planet and two other planets. No one, in the history of time, has come close to doing what you have managed to do in such a short amount of time. We wanted to acknowledge this," the face went on to say, "There is a gift for you Jake, it's only for you, no one else can use it."

"Far out, what do we call you," Jake didn't care about a gift he was more concerned with Archie.

"We don't have a name. Although your bi-pedal kind seems to have a fascination with names... We are one and that's all. We took this form to communicate with you," the face said.

"Ok... I guess we will call you... the face," Jake said sarcastically, "Is there something else," Jake asked.

"No, we are finished; you need to find your gift on your land. We aren't sure where it landed but it's there," The face disappeared, and Archie came back to life. They were at full speed and Archie had no idea what had just happened.

"Archie you okay," Jake was a little worried.

"I'm great why do you ask," Archie responds.

"Oh...Never mind let's just get home," Jake didn't feel like explaining. He just wanted some time to digest what just happened. The guys weren't talking they just sat quietly during the ride home. Archie tried to bring up some subjects, but the guys just sat there quietly.

Jake finally said to Archie, "Look we're tired and need rest."

Archie said, "Why don't you sleep."

"Oh. Okay... Sometimes humans rest by sitting quietly," said Archie.

"Okay... Archie quietly," Jake snapped.

After crossing through the portal and back in our galaxy. It was a very quiet three-hour ride back to the ranch. Once safely

on the ground and home. They guys unloaded. Then right to the
bar in the barn. They had a few beers and some shots. Everyone
was in the drinking. Jake, Casey, Tech, Sam, Rusty, June, Vicki,
Ivan and Kateryna joined in. It wasn't quiet anymore.

Jake said, starting with Casey, "What did you see."

"I saw a big face. A white old man beard white hair,"
Casey claimed.

"Ok that's what I saw too," Jake agreed.

"I saw a big black old man with a beard and gray hair,"
Sam said.

"Archie claims there's no gap in his memory," *Archie
can hear and see everything Jake can, as long as Jake has his
ear pods in.* Jake was thinking through what happened today,
"Were we hypnotized or did that entity project straight into our
brains? Could he have bridged Archie's memory? Maybe he
froze time… No, we were drifting, if time were frozen then the
car would be stopped," Jake was racing through the possibilities.

"I don't know what to think," Sam said.

"I do. You met God," said Kateryna very nervously.

"You know… she might be right," said Jake. He was
trying to calm her down. But that didn't help she was getting
upset. June comforted her and told Jake to shut it.

Casey smiled, "No, this thing has better technology than
us. We must operate keeping that in mind or we're defeated
before we get started. Tech we can beat."

Everyone started to relax by having a few more shots
and beers.

"What's the plan?" June asked.

"No plan, now we drink, tomorrow we plan," Jake
announced.

Written By
J.R. Wilson

The Adventures of
Jake & Archie

The next morning everyone was sporting a hangover. After they had breakfast and ate at least one aspirin a piece. The vitamin B12 was taken as well... a little late for some. Jake was feeling better and had an idea. He went to the barn. Archie mentioned he was getting a strange reading about fifty yards from the back of the barn.

Jake and Sam were trying to get past the hangover and walked to where Archie was getting those strange readings. There was a spear lying on the ground Jake picked it up and it was light as a feather. He threw it at a tree it went through the tree and into the one behind it.

"Wow," said Sam, "let me try," Sam tried and tried but couldn't pull it out if the tree, "Jake I'm afraid that thing isn't coming out."

Jake went over and grabbed on to the spear and gave it a pull, it came out easy.
Jake said, "Maybe you should work out more," Jake set down the spear and Sam tried to pick it up. But he couldn't.

"What the hell? What is this Thor's hammer," Sam said really aggravated.

"The big face guy said it was meant for me," Jake recalled.

Back in the barn. Jake pushed a small button on the spear. It was reduced to a foot long tube. It acted like an old time telescope the way it reduced in size.

"Archie, can you get a hold of the scientist and find out if they can make a portal to the realm. That way I can meet with him in the realm."

"Sure, that shouldn't be a problem." Archie answered. Archie went to work trying to get through to the scientists. Jake went over to the couch and laid down.

Written By
J.R. Wilson

The Adventures of
Jake & Archie

About an hour later Archie told Jake, he managed to get a hold of the scientist, they are working on a new portal. Later that day Archie got a transmission the scientist had completed the portal.

Jake asked Archie, "Can you tell them to meet me there in a few minutes?"

Archie got in contact, and they said, "We will see you in the realm," he asked them to meet Jake at the house.

Jake went into Archie's trunk and opened his portal. Jake went down the stairs. When Jake arrived in the house the scientists were waiting for him, "We ran into a very odd alien on our way home in your galaxy," Jake continued to tell the whole story and at the same time showing them the spear.

"This isn't from here. I've never seen metal like this," the scientist had to run tests on the metallurgy. After running all the tests he could. The scientists announced, "This is from another planet or galaxy. It shouldn't even exist."

"So… he said he had been watching you on earth as well as the Coot and our planet? How is that even possible," The scientist remarked.

"I have a hunch that it can't leave your galaxy. We need a plan to deal with this. I don't think it has portal technology," Jake declared.

"We can make you guys helmets with lining that mental powers can't penetrate," The scientist offered.

"That would be great! Get ahold of Archie when you're done. I think meeting in the realm; this way could become a habit," Jake was glad they were helping. He climbs the stairs into Archie's trunk. He told the news to the guys.

Written By
J.R. Wilson

The Adventures of
Jake & Archie

"We need a plan to deal with this entity," Casey was trying to figure out what to do, "If we have helmets that stop the entity from getting in our heads. We are halfway there. What can we defeat him with? And is he watching or listening to us now," Casey pointed out.

"We will have to risk it and assume he can hear us," Jake said.

"What's first after we get our helmets," Tech asked.

"With the helmets we go on a trip to Amorlites planet. On our usual path. Pretend everything is normal," Jake laid out a simple plan, so they can think on their feet if something unexpected happens. He knew they needed to be flexible. Archie got a message from the scientists. The head scientist said the helmets are ready and he would leave them outside the house in the realm. Jake is back in Archie's trunk. Once in the house Jake went outside and collected the helmets. Jake came out of the trunk with helmets in hand.

"You think they will fit," Casey asked, "Well we try them on and swap them until we find our size."

"The scientist has our sizes," Jake confirmed all is going to plan.

They tried them on, and the helmet adjusted to fit on its own.

"We're ready, I guess," Jake said, "Who's coming?"

Sam wanted to come, and Casey really didn't want to go back so soon. Tech, and Rusty were in. They wanted some action. The four of them loaded up and said their goodbyes.

Archie backed out and said, "Hit the green button."

Jake laughed and said, "It's done."

They took off like they were shot out of a canon. Archie wanted to get this over with. He wasn't sure what happened on the last trip. But he was going to find out on this trip.

Written By
J.R. Wilson

The Adventures of
Jake & Archie

"We are getting close to where we launch the portal," Archie informed everyone.

"Archie, hold on. Wait don't start that portal, turn around we're going back! Casey was right about having helmets. We are halfway there. Halfway isn't enough. What were we thinking… halfway has never been enough," Jake explained.

He had an epiphany. He was letting everything push him in one direction. He needed to sit down and think of why he cares about going after this entity. When all it did was give him a gift and praised his work. Archie turned around. The guys were wondering but they knew Jake and trusted him completely. They went along without question.

"You want to know the plan," Jake snapped, "Well here it is, we go home we fire up the BBQ. Then they drink and eat. Tomorrow is Saturday. June and I go to breakfast at the café. We get back to our normal, so we can get back some perspective. I'm burned out and need to take a couple days off!"

The guys agreed let's get away from all the crazy so we can recharge. These humans never stop surprising Archie. Jake gets angry with him every time he shows Jake a new feature. They are coming into the atmosphere. Everything is good Archie hates getting heated up. He comes in slow. But they make it back to the ranch in one piece.

"What? Why? Your home what happened," June was hugging Jake. She went on, "It doesn't matter your home! Let's fire up the grill," June hollered the guys unloaded Archie. Then fired up the BBQ. It's a big BBQ it can cook for twenty people and only use half the grill.

Jake glanced at June, "Remember breakfast at the café," she smiled.

"Of course… I'm not the one who forgets."

Written By
J.R. Wilson

The Adventures of
Jake & Archie

"Maybe we hit the store pick up a few things," Jake liked making June happy.

" What happened Jake," June asked.

He began to tell her the whole story and just wanted to get away from it all for a bit.

She looked at him and said, "Good you're supposed to be retired," he had been getting her in danger. Everyone needs a break.

In the morning, Jake and June climbed into Archie and headed into town.

"Let's see if the sheriff has had breakfast," Jake suggested.

June said, "Sounds good. I like him, he's good people."

"Yeah, I need some good people around lately. I don't know what to think, aliens, weird entity, Ukrainians and Russians," Jake just wanted to recharge or reboot. *Re... something.* They pull up to the sheriff's office. Jake runs in to see if the sheriff is hungry. Jake and the sheriff come out, together and they all go to the café.

When they entered as usual Susan, June's sister, greeted and seated them. She is always glad to see the sheriff. Susan has a thing for the sheriff. The three of them sat drinking coffee. June brings up the President making Jake a U.S. Marshall in person.

"Let me see the badge," the sheriff was happy for Jake. He stood up and yelled, "Attention everyone! I have an announcement to make."

"Stand up Jake," June told him with nudge. Jake stood up.

Written By
J.R. Wilson

The Adventures of
Jake & Archie

The sheriff continued, "I figure this is as good a place as any looking around the room… I can see that the whole town will know by lunchtime. The President of these United States made Jake a U. S. Marshall for being such a big help to the President."

Now the café holds two hundred people and it's a very large restaurant. Everyone applauded.

Jake looked around and said, "Everyone in here, breakfast is on me!" Then everyone really applauded. Jake laughed, "Oh, now you applaud."

When they sat down their food came. In the corner was a guy, just passing through, talking to his waitress, "I'll pay for my own breakfast. I don't know this guy and could care less he's a U.S. Marshall," with that he got up walked over to Jake's table and said, "I don't know who you think you are, buying everyone breakfast, I'm not impressed."

Jake stood up while wiping his mouth with the napkin in his right hand. The troublemaker threw an overhand right, and Jake caught it with his left hand. He started squeezing the guy's hand till he dropped to his knees and was begging Jake to stop. Jake let go and you could see the troublemakers' hand swelling.

"What do we do with this guy sheriff? Should we arrest him for assault on a U.S. Marshall?"

"I don't know it's a lot of paperwork," the sheriff said half laughing.

People in the café were saying "arrest him, we saw he tried to hit you."

"Yeah, arrest him."

Jake looked around and said, "He really didn't assault me. I caught him in mid assault, so he's just inept and probably embarrassed and I have to take my wife to the store. So… maybe next time," everybody half laughed and applauded.

Written By
J.R. Wilson

The Adventures of
Jake & Archie

The sheriff escorted the troublemaker out of the café.
Then he came back to finish his breakfast. Jake got up and went
over to Susan, and they went into the kitchen,
"Susan how much do you think we got out there?"
"Oh, it's probably four thousand dollars," she said.
"Okay here," he handed her about forty-five hundred
dollars.
Susan said, "You own the café... why are you paying?"
Jake grinned and said, "I said breakfast was on me. I
didn't say it was on the house."
Susan nodded, she understood. Jake and June made
Susan the manager two years ago. She liked Running the place
and was good at it. Jake paid everyone a good wage all he tried
to do was break even. But that little café made money. It was a
win-win. Jake and June continued their trip around town.
After they went to the store. Jake had Archie go stealth
and take off. They flew over the little town. They talked about
making plans, the kind of stuff they like to do, and adding
something new to the town. Maybe get some gravel roads
paved. While they were talking. Jake kept thinking about that
damn entity. What is his goal and what he wants?

Written By
J.R. Wilson

The Adventures of
Jake & Archie

Chapter 27
The Boys Are Back In Town

They went back to the ranch. As they approached, they saw a familiar-looking Jeep.

"Jamie's here," June hollered. She's very excited. They landed and started unloading and Jamie came out to help. Lots of hugs and kisses.

"Jamie your hurt," June observed, "Why the sling?"

"I'll tell you about it when we get your groceries inside," Jamie answered.

Once inside, everyone was there and wanted to know what happened to Jamie. First Jake introduced Jamie to Ivan and Kateryna. Jamie started to tell his story.

"We were on a mission all I can say is we were under attack. In country I can't divulge. My guys were pinned down. I couldn't get to 'em. I started tossing grenades and couple smoke grenades and anti-personal grenades. I shot a couple of times and made my move. I was running to my men when I caught one in shoulder it knocked me down, but I kept rolling and shooting until I was near enough to throw myself in the trench with my men two were wounded. I couldn't see a way out. I guess I kind of lost it, I don't remember my men said."

"I started picking the attackers off one by one. I would take a quick look. Duck, move and raise up take the shot. Then move down the bank look, duck, move then raise up and shoot again. I kept this up for about twenty minutes and realizing there was no more shooting. One of my wounded men and I helped each other to safety. Once he was safe, I went back and carried

Written By
J.R. Wilson

the last of my men out. I was hit and caught one in the leg just as we were getting back to safety. I pulled my side arm and killed that shooter. Turns out I was hit twice."

"The helicopter wouldn't come in because the Landing zone was hot. This is the funny part. My radio man told them, 'Its Jamie!' The operator on the other end said, 'We will be there in ten minutes.' They picked me and my two wounded men up. I thought the chopper was taking too many hits, but that pilot got us back to base. The Chopper was riddled with bullet holes. We were so lucky."

"When I got out of the hospital. The admiral called me in. Jamie, you're one of the best commanders I've got. You know, you took out twelve of the enemies that day. You saved two of your men while you were wounded. amazing stuff.' The admiral continued. 'Now you have a decision to make. You can stay in, you will be on a desk, or you can go out on disability.' It didn't take me more than New York Minute. To take the disability. Three grand a month. I decided to come home and work with pops." Jamie explained, "The admiral gave me these."

Jamie pulled eight little boxes from his bag. Metals one of the boxes had two purple hearts. The other boxes had, navy cross, distinguish service. Expert rifle and one for pistol there were a couple others for action he was in. "The admiral said they don't give these metals while you're serving," said Jamie. The moment flashed back to the conversation for him as he continued the story.

"It can be difficult, explaining where you earned them, it's all top secret so I kept them in my safe. You earned them and I wanted to make sure you received your metals. Jamie, sorry there's no big ceremony," said the admiral.

Written By
J.R. Wilson

"That's okay, I will miss the marines and thanks for all you've done for me sir," said Jamie.

"No! No! Your country thanks you, Jamie," replied the admiral.

"I'm sure Connie is happy," added June. It brought Jamie back to the moment.

"She doesn't know… I didn't want any of you to worry. I didn't tell anyone." Jamie reported, "Here mom put these somewhere, please." As he tried to hand her the boxes, June was hugging her son and very happy he was in, one piece.

Jake said, "As long as your alive and home it's all good. Even if you lost both legs, as long as you are alive, we can deal with it."

Jamie laughed, "Pops is that okay, can I work for you?"

Jake gave his boy a hug and said, "Are you kidding? I wouldn't have it any other way," Jake started to fill in Jamie on what they have been up to and the entity.

"I don't understand what it wants," Jamie inquired.

"That's the sixty-thousand-dollar question… we don't know. I want to go back and find out. I just can't get myself to kill an alien when all he did was complement our work and give me a gift. It has an agenda. We just haven't figured it out."

"Pop, if we go back… and I say 'we' because I'm coming with you. If we go back… can we beat this thing," Jamie just wanted to know what their chances are.

"Archie seems to think we can. He's usually right," Jake assured him.

"When do we leave," Jamie was ready to go.

"We are in no hurry we need a plan. We have our helmets, the scientists made for us to keep the entity out of our heads," Jake went on to say, "Besides, you need to get healed up and I might know how to help."

Written By
J.R. Wilson   197

The Adventures of
Jake & Archie

"Let's get to Archie's trunk. We are going for a visit," Jake announced.

"Hey Jake, I have question that's been bugging me," Rusty asked, "Why can we go through Archie's portal and not have to phase?"

"Well… the way it was explained to me is Archie's portal is small. It doesn't join to another galaxy, just the realm. The realm is not affected by time, and we only need to take a couple steps to go through. When we slip through to change galaxies it's larger and if we didn't phase and slip through, we would die. The paradox we create goes out five hundred thousand miles. That's why we must be in deep space, away from planets. We never want to cause time disruption. That's about all I know. I'm not an expert." Jake finished up.

They walked through the realm to get to the portal the Amorlites created that leads to their planet. When they passed through. It turns out, it comes out in the lab. The scientists were glad to see Jake, his son, and his men.

"Why the visit Jake? Can we help you? Wait your son is injured… let us help," The head scientist picked up on his injury.

"That's why we're here. We would appreciate any help you can give," Jake was happy they could help.

The scientist came over to Jamie and said, "Sit down here, I need a small blood sample Jamie."

Then he pricked Jamie's arm with the end of the healing wand. Jake noticed when the commander used the wand on his navigator, while they were at Jakes house. Theres a tube that runs the length of the wand, it glowed green, but now it glows red.

"Why does the wand glow red now," Jake asked.

Written By
J.R. Wilson

The Adventures of
Jake & Archie

The scientist answered, "Your race has red blood not green. We always match the blood type and DNA."

"Do you have one of those you can spare. I would like to keep one of those in Archie just in case," Jake requested.

"You can have this one, as soon as I'm done," the scientist didn't mind giving Jake some healing abilities, "Now hold still," The scientist instructed Jamie.

He waved the wand back and forth for about two minutes over Jamie's leg and then started on his shoulder again for two minutes. Jamie's leg healed and it didn't leave a scar. His shoulder healed right up.

"That's amazing," Jamie couldn't believe this worked, no more pain he was moving his shoulder, and it didn't hurt.

"Great now let's talk about the entity," Jake requested.

The scientist started filling in Jake on all they found out sense his last visit, "We believe the entity came from the realm. we can't determine how or when it arrived," said the scientist, "We are continuing our research. Here you can have this," he handed Jake the wand.
The scientist explained how it works to Jake.

"Hey," Jake came out of nowhere, "You guys are building another car," the scientist nodded, "What are you going to do with it," Jake was puzzled the scientists weren't more forth coming about the car.

"We are trying out new systems and made it for deep space travel," the scientist wasn't telling Jake everything, Jake could tell.

Jake changes the subject, "So the planet we use in the realm is where it came from," Jake guessed.

"No, I don't think it's from that particular planet. We believe it comes from the realm, more than likely another planet in the realm. We don't know which one."

Written By
J.R. Wilson

"Sounds like you're getting close. We will wait before we do anything, I still have a problem. I can't go after someone or something, who compliments me for my work and gives me a gift. That spear… I don't know how to classify this situation. Is the entity friend or foe," Jake was not sure how to proceed, "If the entity would attack or threaten us, anything hostile I would know what to do."

They said their goodbyes and went back into the realm. When Jake and guys were home. Jake stashed the wand in Archie's trunk.

"All this seems so unreal. We may need to bring an assortment of weapons on our next trip and maybe a few surprises," Jake wants to be ready for anything, "Rusty, you and Casey need to come up with some super weapons. I don't know what, I'll leave that up to you. Remember whatever you come up with has to work in deep space," Jake requested.

"You got it boss. We will come with something radical," Rusty said confidently.

Jake and Archie were talking, "Hey Jake, do you think the entity found my portal in the realm. Maybe that's how he came into this galaxy."

"That would make sense he can probably go through the smaller portal like us. But not in the larger one where he has to phase," Jake speculated, "What if we found the portal? Maybe we could… I don't know, maybe Archie could lock on his beam and send the entity through, sending it home. What do you think Archie?"

"That might work if we can lock it on, and if we can beam it into the stasis, and if we can beam it through the portal, and if, where we send him… is home… that's a lot of 'if's'," said Archie.

Jake and Jamie were laughing.

Written By
J.R. Wilson

The Adventures of
Jake & Archie

Written By
J.R. Wilson

Chapter 28
The Search And Rescue

"Hey Jake, I'm getting a call," said Archie.

"Put it through Archie," said Jake.

"Hey, pops you there?"

"Tony what's the good word," Jake was happy to hear from his other son.

"I'm coming home. I'm on the road and about thirty minutes out."

"Great I'll tell your mom," Jake was excited. He ran in the house and told June.

"Oh my God! I need to fix some dinner he will be hungry," June was so happy she was doing her happy dance. Jake was laughing. He loved it when June does her happy dance, "Everyone will be home. This is all I ever wanted," June was bursting.

Tony pulls in and parks. Jamie and Jake Walk out to meet him. Lots of hugs June ran out and slammed into Tony hugging and kissing him. Even Bullet ran out to see Tony and jumped up on him.

"Good boy, you're such a good boy Bullet," Tony was petting Bullet with both hands.

"Come in I made some dinner," June announced.

Over dinner everyone was there. Tony started talking, "I have an announcement. I put in my papers. After talking to Jamie and realizing he was right. I want to come home and work for pop. Jamie and I talked about this when he got out of the hospital. I just hadn't decided yet. But it didn't take me long.

Written By
J.R. Wilson

Plus I was wounded a lot. They put me out as disabled, I got that going for me, which is nice," everyone laughed. Tony liked making Bill Murray impressions. I am a big *Caddie Shack* fan.

"What's on the agenda?" Tony asks with his mouth full.

"Well, we have an unusual situation there's an entity in the Amorlites galaxy," Jake explained everything including having issues with not wanting to hurt or kill something that hasn't done any harm, it even gave Jake a gift.

"In other words, this isn't a run in and kick butt kind of deal," Tony replied.

"No, we are working on a plan. We think he came here from another galaxy… possibly the realm and can't get home. But this is speculation. We need to go back to be sure," Jake filling in Tony.

"What we need to find is Archie's old portal. Then maybe we can send the entity back to his home. But again it's all speculation."

Tony butts in, "Why not send a few of us into the realm to search for the portal? While we're doing that you can go and confront the entity. If its willing, we help, if it's not we toast him."

"Good I'm liking that plan maybe Archie can get a hold of the scientist and see if they have a device to locate the portal plus some communication so we can all stay in contact," Jake was getting into that old planning mode.

They finished supper and went out to the barn. Jake was still figuring out how to approach this. Archie was sending signals to the scientists. They finally responded. They would have everything the searchers will need to locate the lost portal.

"Here's the plan at this point. Tony you, Tech, Casey, and Rusty get your gear together you're going into the realm. Sam, Jamie, and I will meet the entity and see what's up. We

Written By
J.R. Wilson

will have to adjust on the fly from there," Jake continues,
"When you get in the realm make your way to the other portal
that one leads to the scientist's lab. They will have devices to
help with the search. Also see if they have a tracker. We may
need it. You can't move the portal, only Archie can beam it to
his stasis. So throw the tracker into the portal then Archie can
find it from the galaxy side."

"Sounds good if everything comes together," Jamie
agreed.

June came out the barn, "Are you leaving tonight," June
asked.

"No, we will hit it in the morning," Jake replied.

"Sounds good I will make sure y'all get breakfast first,"
June said.

The next morning, "Something smells great," Tony said,
while coming out of his bedroom.

"Breakfast is ready," June announced.

Everyone was sitting and enjoying biscuits and gravy,
taters, and eggs. "Wow, you really did it right fixing pop's
favorite," Jamie's said.

It was his favorite too. After breakfast Jake had a few
things to say, "Okay… everyone make sure you're wearing the
buckles I bought for you when I retired. Huh… retired maybe I
should rephrase that. Remember these have trackers in them,"
Jake had these made for the whole family which include Casey,
Tech, and Rusty. He knew his retirement would have challenges
and old enemies trying to find him.

Tony, Tech, Rusty, and Casey crawled into Archies
portal, and they were off to the scientist's lab. Jake, Jamie, and
Sam loaded up into Archie. They took off for the Amorlites
galaxy.

Written By
J.R. Wilson   204

The Adventures of
Jake & Archie

Jake was talking to Sam and Jamie, "Okay I'm going to tell y'all the secret to life. This is besides being helpful and giving. The secret is… first, always be on time. Ten minutes early is on time. Second, always do what you say you will do. In other words, don't say you will do something and not do it. Third, try not to make promises. They are hard to keep… but if you're sure then take that risk. If you live by this your life will be much easier to manage. That's it," Jake said, "No guru no complicated stuff to remember. Oh yeah… my dad tries telling me about women, but he admitted he didn't know much. He had been with your grandma. For as long as your mom and I. Grandpa and grandma also met when they were kids… I guess the lesson here is if you find a good one, hang on, don't give up, and treat her right. That's it, hope it helps you in the future," Jake concluded.

"Thanks Pop. You know you have told that to me before… about a hundred times before," Jamie laughed.

"I told it for Sam's benefit."

Sam smiled, "That's okay a little motivation."

"When I'm gone and you're fifty. You will remember these stories, and you will do the same for your kids. Bore them with rerun stories. That's how they stick, and you remember," said Jake.

"We are approaching the portal location," Archie reported. Archie went into phase mode, and they slipped through to the Amorlites galaxy. Jamie was amazed that space had so many colors, especially the nebulas.

"This is so cool Pop, you do this a lot," asked Jamie.

"We do what is required. Personally… I find space very lonely. I said it before, and I'll say it again, there is no way I could be an astronaut," Jake insisted.

Written By
J.R. Wilson

The Adventures of
Jake & Archie

"Pop… you are an astronaut. You have taken more trips and gone further than any astronauts at NASA. Plus, you have been in battles in space. NASA is years away from battling anyone in space," Jamie was bragging on his dad.

"Ok fine, but I'm not wearing those stupid suits," Jake laughed, "I guess we should put on the helmets."

Sam and Jamie were having fun laughing at Jake's expense, "No suits but these helmets are ok." Jamie and Sam laughing.

Mean time Tony and the guys have just left the scientist's lab. They have a few goodies including a tracker to help lead them to the lost portal. Tony tried raising his dad in the communication devices the scientists gave them.

"Pops you copy," Tony spoke.

"Got ya son you are loud and clear," Jake responded.

"Great. We are on our way in to search for the portal the scientists were very helpful and a bit funny looking," Tony laughed.

Jake was laughing with him, "Yeah, but they are a great bunch. See you when we see you. We're clear," Jake signed off.

Tony had the tracker on, and it looked like something around two miles away, "Let's head in this direction looks like maybe a couple miles or so."

Back on-board Archie, Jamie was freaked when he put on the helmet, "This thing grabbed my head. Is that how it works," he wondered.

Written By
J.R. Wilson

The Adventures of
Jake & Archie

Jake smiled and said, "The scientists made them one size fits all. They had our sizes. They figured this would work better and they were right."

Archie spoke up, "We are getting close to the place we ran into the entity."

"Ok, Archie start scanning for anything no matter how small," Jake ordered.

"I'm picking up something but it's about a hundred miles down below us," Archie reported.

"Head for it Archie, get as close as you can," Jake replied.

"What is it," Sam asked.

"Looks like a triangle but it's so small. It's about half the size of Archie," Sam continues, "Can that be the thing we were worried about?"

Archie lined up on it no more than a hundred yards away, "Hey boss, we're getting a message over my receiver."

"Put it through," Jake commanded.

"I will destroy you. My shields are strong you won't be able to penetrate them. We are strong!"

"Hello, can you hear me," Jake asked, "We don't want to hurt you."

"Is that you Jake," the entity asked.

"It sure is," Jake responded.

"Why couldn't I see you coming," the entity was confused.

"We have protective helmets so you couldn't access or minds. That's very disturbing for our kind we would rather talk," Jake informed it, "What is your intent toward us. You know your goal in the big picture. We don't want to fight we want to help you. We believe you're stuck in our universe. Is that true," Jake inquired.

Written By
J.R. Wilson

"How did you know? You are very smart. We just want to go home, we are lost," said the entity.

"That's what we thought, we can get you back through the portal. You will have to trust us. We need to beam you into stasis so we can get you back where you belong," Jake explained.

"We trust you. You could have attacked us, but you didn't. Do what's necessary we will trust you," the entity wants to go home badly.

"Archie do your thing let's get it aboard," Jake ordered. Archie locked on and beamed the entity into a stasis mode, "Let's get to the Amorlites planet. Just as fast as you can," Jake wanted to get this over with.

"Okay boss we're moving out. Is the green button active?"

"You know it is," replied Jake.

Just like that, they were flying at just a little slower than light speed.

In the meantime, Tony and the guys are following a signal.

"It appears to be over here," Tech was tracking it now. The group walked over and followed the signal for another hundred yards.

"That must be it, looks like a portal," Rusty pointed out.

"Pops are you there? Do you copy," Tony asked.

"We are here, and I mean that, we have the entity and are almost to the Amorlites planet," Jake responded.

"Great we found the portal," Tony added.

Written By
J.R. Wilson

208

The Adventures of
Jake & Archie

"Good deal now throws the tracker in," Jake directed, "Then head to the scientists lab we will meet you there."

"10-4 pops see you soon," Tony acknowledged.

Approaching the planet Archie navigated to the Lab. While Tony and the rest had about an hour's walk back to the lab portal.

"Looks like it's going to work, as long as Archie can pick up the signal to the lost portal," Sam observed.

"There's the lab. We are going to touch down right next to it," Archie was right on track to land.

"Hey Jake, I'm getting a signal from the tracker should we go there now," Archie asked.

"No! Go to the lab. I want to make sure Tony, and the guys are back before we go. They can't get home without us," Jake pointed out.

"Oh yeah, they need Archie to get home," said Sam. Archie set down near the lab. The crew unloaded and went inside.

"Greetings my friends," Jake was glad to see the scientists, "You guys really came through for my men, thank you," Jake was very grateful.

Pretty soon the lab portal opened, "Here come the adventurers," Sam announced.

"We have the entity in Archie's stasis. As soon as we get him home the better, then Archie will beam the portal into his stasis. Then we will head for home, give us a few hours then we will call and give the okay to come back through the portal at the house," Jake laid it out for all to hear.

"Sounds like you got it figured out," says Jamie, "What are we going to do with the lost portal? Well… I guess we must rename it now," Jamie was laughing.

Written By
J.R. Wilson

The Adventures of
Jake & Archie

"We put it at the ranch it will make things easy when we need to deal with the Amorlites," Jake replied, "Ok let's get this done we will be in contact," Jake commanded.

Tony and the guys were waiting in the lab and made themselves comfortable. It's going to be a few hours. Archie was almost to the lost portal. Once they arrived, they realized how big it was. The commander really stretched it out when he took it from Archie and pulled Archie through it.

"You know… I can drive or fly right through," Archie said a bit surprised.

"So do it, we go through to beam out the entity so he can go home then we fly back through. Beam the portal into stasis and head for home," Jake thought this is a great plan. On the realm side of the portal Archie beamed out the entity.

"Does this look right to you," Jake asked wanting to make sure this is its home.

"Yes, it does. Thank you so much. You are a compliment to your race. If you look straight up, you can see my planet. Come visit us, we welcome friendly visitors. Thanks again," the entity went up and out of sight. Archie marked the planet with his Navigation equipment.

"Maybe we come back one day," Archie said. Archie went out, the way he came in and locked onto the portal and beamed into his stasis. They called Tony and told him they are on their way home. It was an uneventful trip back home.

Jake called Tony and said, "We are in the barn, parked and the trunk is up."

Tony said, "Be a couple minutes, then we will be there," true to his word, the guys came out one by one, "Nice to be back," Tony was feeling tired.

All the guys were tired. June came out with some sandwiches and went over to the bar. She started pouring, ice cold beer from the tap. Coors of course. The sandwiches and the beer brought everyone back to life.

Jake stood up and said, "I think we did good today. We helped another race and now we must determine where the best place for the lost portal that we found... you're right we need a new name for this portal... to be placed safe and Archie has to be able to get to it, and for June and anyone else to escape to. If its ever necessary."

"We can work on that tomorrow," Jake is very tired.

The next day people started getting up, moving around.

"Coffee, we need lots of coffee," June was saying to herself.

Jake and Sam were talking over a cup of coffee.

"I think we need to build a special small barn. It must be secure for the portal. Archie must be able to get in and secure the building before going through the portal," said Jake.

Sam says, "I agree it has to be hidden but easy to access."

Without warning a car comes up the driveway. Jake and Sam Walk out onto the porch to see who gets out. When they see who it is.

Jake says, "Well, well... it's not for us," He laughed.

Connie gets out and when Jamie sees her he comes a running, "Hey you, why didn't you call and tell me you're back," Connie asked a little hurt.

Jamie gave her a hug and kiss, "I was going to call you this morning. I'm so glad you came out to the ranch. I was, oh... never mind," he was going to tell her. He was wounded and sporting a sling when he got home. But after the wand treatment, what's the point?

"Jamie and Connie are so nice together," June was telling Jake.

Written By
J.R. Wilson

The Adventures of
Jake & Archie

"I'm out, no more military for me and I get three grand a month for life. Pretty sweet deal," Jamie was telling Connie.

"Why the money other guys get out and don't get squat," Connie looked at Jamie, "You got hurt didn't you! When were you going to tell me?"

"Yeah, but you don't understand," Jamie started explaining to Connie everything including the wand.

She just stood there, "Show me where you were hurt," Jamie took off his shirt and she couldn't believe how it was all better from a bullet wound, "That's nice your all brand new. What happens when you go in for a checkup, and the doctor can't find any sign of a wound?
You will lose your disability and probably must pay it back," Connie said.

"I will tell the truth and bring in the wand to show them," Jamie replied, "Besides the military has a record of my injuries. You worry too much."

They both laughed. Connie was happy Jamie was home, and in one piece. Jamie was happy because Connie was laughing.

NASA was calling. Archie picked it up, "Hey Jake NASA, is calling it's Jerry."

Jake jumped into Archie, "Jerry what can I do for ya," Jake was thinking. *I really must stop using that phrase.*

"Hi Jake, just checking with you. Are we still good? I haven't heard from you in a while," said Jerry.

"Of course we're good. I've been a little busy, but things are leveling out," Jake was wondering what this call is about, "Jerry what's this call really about?"

"We need help, can you give us a hand with our lunar project," Jerry asked in desperation.

Written By
J.R. Wilson

"Jerry, you sound a little desperate. We just got in from a long trip. Can we talk tomorrow, will whatever it is, wait till then," Jake just wanted some sleep.

"Sure, we can talk tomorrow, sounds good," Jerry agreed.

"Great till then," Jake ended the call.

Chapter 29
NASA Is Calling

The next morning Jake was on his porch drinking his coffee remembering what it once was. He retired, taking it easy. But living life is better. Isn't it?

"Oh well, the old magnet is still working. Both weird and trouble," Jake chuckled to himself.

Jake could hear Archie saying in his ear pods, "NASA is calling Jake. Should I tell them you will call them back?"

"No… put them through," Jake said. Archie can transfer calls to Jake's ear pods.

"Good morning, Jake. You are doing good," Jerry asked.

"Good morning to you, I'm just having my morning coffee," Jake wasn't fully awake and can be testy in the morning.

"Can you come down here I want to show you something," Jerry still sounded desperate.

"Sure, say… around noon and I'll be there," Jake figured something with humans involved. It could be fun. Jamie and Connie were staying occupied, and Sam was at his home with Vicki. They have some catching up to do. Jake asked Tony if he wanted to go to Huston. He was all for it. Archie was ready for a short trip. A chance to see more of the United States and Texas was great place to start.

They were off to Texas. It wasn't long before they were over NASA. Archie set down outside one of the bigger buildings. Jake called Jerry and told him where they were. He directed them to what looked like an airplane hangar. Once Archie pulled up in front the big doors opened. Archie had removed the stealth when he landed. So, he drove in like any other car.

Once inside Jerry came up to them. He invited them inside the inner office to talk, "So what's so urgent," Jake asked trying to be nice.

"We have a lunar project, and we need to build a complex on the moon," Jerry kept on, "I need you to take me up there to survey an area."

"Is that all, why didn't you just come out and say so on the phone," Jake didn't mind this for him it's like running to 7/11.

Tony was ecstatic, "Going to the moon dang-o this is a great day!"

Jerry joined them in Archie. Archie engaged stealth and they were off. Of course, Jake hit the green button. They were at sub light speed, so it only took about a half hour to get to the moon. Too bad we can't get out and check out the moon. Jake said jokingly, and Jerry was beside himself.

"We're right above the moon," exclaimed Jerry.

"You can get out and walk around all you want," Archie announced.

"What? How? No space suits no air," Jake said abruptly.

"I just wrap you with a protective shield you can breathe, you need to worry about heat or cold. The shield will protect you up to a hundred yards then it starts to fade. Just stay around seventy yards or less and you will be fine," Archie stated.

"There's another tid bit you could have brought up sooner," Jake says. Okay he would check out the moon's surface with Jerry. Archie landed, Jerry and Jake just stared at each other. Who goes first? Jake opened the door. He figured it didn't matter once you open the door you're both committed. Nothing happened, no rushing air, no dying.

"Jake, now there's a bubble over the car. It goes out thirty feet from me," Archie explained. Then the wrap will kick in as you leave the bubble you should stop around seventy yards."

"Wow that's amazing," Jerry was really freaking out. They looked at some level areas. Took pictures and some measurements. Then loaded up, Tony was enjoying the moon. He wanted to stay for a while. He knew he couldn't. They took off for earth. Jerry was telling Jake about the structure; he wanted Jake to see the plans. When they landed Jerry took them into planning area. Jerry was going on and on about the structure.

Jake asked, "Archie can you construct a portal from earth to the moon?"

"Probably… it could work. You won't even have to phase," said Archie.

"That would be fantastic. We have a full-scale model," said Jerry.

"Wait? What? You have a full-scale model," Jake couldn't believe his luck, "Wait on the portal. Okay!"

He and Archie along with Jerry and Tony. They flew according to Jerry's direction to the location of the full-scale model. Arriving and hovering overhead.

Written By
J.R. Wilson

The Adventures of
Jake & Archie

Jake ask, "Why didn't you tell me sooner? Does it work is it functional," Jake asked. Mildly upset everyone not being up front.

"Yes we had astronauts training there they lived in it for a month," Jerry said.

"We have to disassemble it for transport to the moon," Jerry informed Jake.

Jake was shaking his head, "You should have told me this up front. We can transport that to the moon today," Jake informed Jerry.

"You can? Oh wow, what do I need to do," Jerry asked.

"Sit back and enjoy the ride. Archie are you ready," Jake asked, "Let's do this thing." Archie was wound up to get finished. Archie beams the structure to his stasis. Then he turned his attention to the moon. They took off. Archie was trying to make good time, they were over the moon in about a half hour.

"Where do you want it," Archie inquired.

"There! Over there, where its level and far enough from where the servicing rockets will land and take off from," Jerry was giving the instructions. Archie beamed it right where Jerry wanted.

"So that should save NASA time and money," Jake pointed out.

"Yes, this is great. Let's go back I might have one littler chore for Archie," Jerry hinted around. When they were back over NASA, "We some supplies we need on the moon. They are all in that warehouse," Jerry was hoping Archie could pull this off.

"We beam it to Archie's stasis and head back for the moon. Sound about right there, Jerry?" Jake confirmed what he wanted.

"You got it Jake," Jerry was very happy.

Written By
J.R. Wilson

The Adventures of
Jake & Archie

"Any problems with this Archie," Jake was just checking.

"We are good to go," Archie stated and beam up the supplies.

They started back to the moon. Archie was close to the moon. But he didn't need to go all the way back just to beam some supplies. He went ahead and beamed everything down. Keeping a good distance from the rocket pad as he did before. He beams it to the opposite side of the moon house they delivered earlier.

"All done," Jake asked Jerry.

"All done, let's go back," Jerry couldn't believe what they accomplished. In one day, they did what would have taken many, many months, maybe even a year or two for NASA to complete. When they landed. Jerry's crew came out and applauded. It really made their day.

"When do we start on the portal," one of the crew asked.

"We decided not at this time," Jerry said, "Thanks to Archie and Jake we did what the portal would have."

Jake chimed in, "Yes, if we build a portal, the attacks on this facility would be endless. Foreign governments, criminals, sabotage. It would be a nightmare. If you want help, call me."

"We can haul supplies and personal up there. But aren't you supposed to use your rockets? It might be a bit suspicious. If all this gets done and you haven't fired a rocket," Jake was pointing out the hazards. Remember top, top secret everybody has to understand how important this is, keeping all this quiet," Jake repeats this to impact the workers.

"Let's go home Archie boy," Jake couldn't wait to get home, "The guys should be working on the building for the portal," Jake was hoping. When he arrived at the ranch he found

Written By
J.R. Wilson

218

the building framed and everyone is working, "Wow, you guys are really getting it built. Good job all."

Jake was thinking he would take everyone out for dinner, "What do you think should we all go out for dinner," Jake asked.

"Wait, no let me make dinner for you." Ivan was very intent on making some food for Jakes family.

"That sounds good to me," June said, "But you have to let me take you to the store. You cook and I'll buy."

"Very good," said Ivan. Kateryna wanted to go she needed things at the store. Kateryna had a list for Ivan.

"We will be back soon." June said.

Ivan wanted to talk to Jake, "Mr. Jake I noticed there is no exotic food restaurants in town. Is there a reason that you know," Ivan said with thick Ukrainian accent.

"No reason it's just no one has opened one because there hasn't been anyone here who cooks exotic food. Heck, I don't think anyone knows what exotic food is. It's not, you know dirty is it," Jake was trying to understand him.

"No maybe I used the wrong... expression? Did I say that right," Ivan replied.

"Yep, that's right. What kind of food are you talking about," Jake was curious.

Ivan tried to explain, "Soups, stews, Borscht, chicken Kyiv, Varenyky, Cabbage rolls. Do you think it would do well here?"

"Do you know how to run a restaurant Ivan," Jake needed to get some background.

"Oh yes. We had our own restaurant for fifteen years. Until the war and they closed us," Ivan was so proud it was easy to see.

Written By
J.R. Wilson

The Adventures of
Jake & Archie

"Well maybe we could help. You need to find a location in our little town. I know all the commercial buildings. . . we may have to build," Jake said.

"Oh… No… we can't afford to build," Ivan said.

Jake said, "I can afford it. We would be partners if you run the restaurant and I'll supply the building and model it anyway you feel comfortable with. Maybe a theme from your country. I will get my architect to draw up whatever you want."

"Oh, Mr. Jake that is so too much," Ivan said in a unique way.

"No problem it will give you and your wife a project. Believe me it will keep you busy," Jake smiled.

"Ok, then partners," Ivan put his hand out to shake. Jake shook hands and gave Ivan a pat on the shoulder.

"To a long partnership," Jake said he was very happy. He was thinking another restaurant he would own half. As long as Ivan is successful Jake won't take any money from his new venture. He will roll it over and put it back into the restaurant. Jake walked back to the new building. The guys were working very hard.

"Guess, I'm going into business with Ivan and Kateryna. Another restaurant this one is going to be different, hopefully people will enjoy," Jake announced.

"It will do great, as soon as they try Ivan's cooking its excellent," Casey was excited for Ivan.

About a week later the building was finished. Jake had Archie beam the portal into the far end of the new building. Jake liked the new building it was large enough for Archie to go in secure the door and enter the portal. It was about five foot longer than Archie. So he had room to come and go without anyone knowing.

Written By
J.R. Wilson

The Adventures of
Jake & Archie

Ivan met Jake's architect, and they began designing the new restaurant. Everything was going smoothly. While Jake was outside hanging with Archie. Enjoying the day. That's when it happened. From out of the blue sky came a half dozen alien ships with hostile intent.

Jake and Archie made a move to take off. Explosions were all around them. They managed to get up in the air and Archie started firing.

"This is not good," said Jake, "Who are these guys do you know, Archie?"

"No idea," said Archie.

Then a shot hit close to Archie and threw the car down. Hitting hard on the ground. Jake was thrown around in Archie. He didn't get a chance to hit the green button. What is going to happen? An attack on the ranch. Unknown attackers. Jake is thrown around.

TO BE CONTINUED

Written By
J.R. Wilson